ASTORIA

STEAK

DELUXE!

A MYSTERY

ASTORIA STEAK DELUXE!

A MYSTERY

BY

JIM HALLAUX

ISBN: 9798679958197

Published in the USA.

1st printing September 2020

29 28 27 26 25 24 23 22 21

Cover art and book interior by Calvin Cahail

Oak and author picture by Robbie Mattson

THIS ONE IS FOR

OAK

WHO IS RARELY CRITICAL

OF MY WORK.

ALSO BY JIM HALLAUX

WIND WITHOUT RAIN   (WITH CALVIN CAHAIL)

ACKNOWLEDGEMENTS

Many thanks to the people that helped with this project;

Robbie Mattson, Larry Helligso, Lorell Stoneman, Phillip Holeman, Alan Robitsch, Paula Gaspari, Clark Tanner, Paul Wenzel, Patty Skinner, Dea Helligso, Dawn Ficken, Larry Lockett, Wes and Rosemary Ginther.

Special thanks to Calvin Cahail and all the staff at Sabretooth Book Services.

CAST OF CHARACTERS

STEAK DELUXE! STAFF

Chef - Chef/Owner

Charlie – Manager

Bernie – Bar Manager

Maylen – Pastry Chef

Bill – Sous Chef

Cassi – Reception

Marty – Bookkeeper

ASTORIA POLICE DEPARTMENT

Sam Jacobs – Police Chief

Cherry Johnson – Detective

Hal Evans – Senior Patrolman

CAST OF CHARACTERS (Continued)

ASTORIANS

Joe Abrams – Assistant District Attorney

Roger Brock – Astoria City Councilman

Missy Brock – Councilman's wife

'Dining-out is America's number 1 indoor sport.'

Dr. Dominic Nigro

1909 - 1992

Steak Deluxe! Restaurant

Astoria, Oregon – 2019

THE CHEF HAS BEEN DRINKING steadily since 3pm; now at 8pm, he's worked himself to sober.

> "One more time Juan, one more time and you're shit-canned. Out of here".

"I'm working on it Chef, almost there__"

"You're almost gone, goddammit. Where is the fish on ticket 22? I've got meat, I've got pasta, where the hell is the fish?"

"Walking it, Chef__"

"Run it Juan, you little incompetent bastard, run it. And then leave, you're fired. Shit-canned, for good."

People who know Chef refer to him as egotistical. Those who know him well, refer to him as an egotistical asshole.

1

THE FIRST THING TO KNOW is that a restaurant is a living (and sometimes dying) organism.

In a restaurant, the kitchen, dining room and bar are 3 separate things. But all part of the same organism.

First, the kitchen. It is the most important part of the restaurant, but the customer never sees it, 'Chef's Table' aside. And a 'Chef's Table' isn't part of the kitchen; it's part of the dining room that has been misplaced. At Steak Deluxe! the kitchen day starts early. At the earliest, there is peace and quiet. The first of the kitchen staff arrives around 8am with a McDonald's coffee in one hand and a pack of cigarettes in the other. Everyone on the kitchen staff smokes.

Juggling keys, smokes and coffee, the man manages to get the kitchen door unlocked. He has a 3-day stubble going on his chin, hair that looks like 'bed-head gone electric,' a grey pallor to his skin. All kitchen staff look like they just got over the flu.

If you are looking for healthy, handsome restaurant workers, look to waiters, especially younger ones.

Additional kitchen staff arrive over the next 30 minutes. With the 5th arrival, the morning crew is complete. They are all men, mostly 20-somethings, a few older, some younger. Almost all of the kitchen staff is Mexican/American; everyone speaks Kitchen/Spanish.

If you are working in a restaurant kitchen, you don't have to speak English and you don't have to speak Spanish. But if you can't understand Kitchen/Spanish, you won't last long. The language is a mixture of English, Spanish, grunts, groans and curse words from both cultures.

There is little talking and less joking among the crew. Everyone has a 'just got up' feeling. The 5 men migrate to their stations, parts of the kitchen they are responsible for. All relish this quiet time. Stoves and flat tops lit, knives sharpened, bar towels acquired and hidden. Bar towels are treasured commodities. If you use someone's knife without asking, there could be a fistfight. If bar towels are pilfered from another workstation, the fight could involve knives.

This morning time is when each station has its *mis en place* (everything in its place) accomplished.

Deliveries begin and everything in the kitchen changes. Quiet time is over; the constant drill of work begins. There are a lot of deliveries; produce, seafood (at Steak Deluxe! it's usually oysters, salmon, shrimp) and meat. The deliveries go to different stations, they are unpacked and the process of turning product into servings starts. That process almost always involves knives, very sharp knives, used in an efficient and surprisingly aggressive manner.

After the various products are broken down into serving sizes, they are placed in areas most accessible to the stations where they will be prepared. Some go on shelves in the walk-in cooler, some in low-boy refrigerators under counters. All meat products at Steak Deluxe! are stored in the famous Steak Locker.

The Steak Locker is part of the operation that the Chef/Owner is most proud. He refers to it as a *'Cathedral of Meat.'* At one end of the walk-in cooler, behind a heavy, locked door is this *'Cathedral.'* Inside is brightly lit, cold and silent, with just a whisper of sound from the ventilation fan. Only 2 staff members have access codes to the Steak Locker; the Chef/Owner and the restaurant manager, Charlie.

Huge sides of beef hang from vicious-looking hooks waiting to be cut into individual servings. On ceiling-high wooden shelves are steaks, tenderloins, chops and enormous tubs of hamburger.

The hamburger at Steak Deluxe goes for $25. Wagyu beef imported from Japan (or so they say) ground in house, with frites fried in duck fat. An enormous onion ring fried the same way. Served on a big platter, frites surrounding burger, topped with the onion ring and a Henckels steak knife stuck upright through the burger. It is the restaurant's best-seller, although profit is lessened by people stealing the knife.

When deliveries are taken care of and stations re-cleaned, its 'Break Time.' The crew heads through the back door; each man fires up a smoke. Most have grabbed a quick couple of puffs already; on the way to the john, in the john or outside taking cartons to the recycling bin. But during morning 'Break,' it's a luxurious, slow, satisfying tobacco/nicotine experience. The dream-like spell is broken when coughing and spitting begin. Cigarettes are accompanied by thick, rich coffee, sometimes with rum added.

With morning break over, cooking begins. Lunch service is fast, the days of a 3-martini lunch, with a steak sandwich thrown in for ballast, ended with the *Great Recession*. Most patrons have an hour for lunch. The menu is short, items prepared in advance and fired last minute. It's a burger, French dip, chef's salad kind of menu, all items made with the freshest ingredients, priced accordingly. Lunch rush begins at 11:30 and ends around 1:30. Patrons, who linger, mostly do so in the bar.

The first ticket comes into the kitchen at 11:45.

> "Ticket number 1, table 6. 2 burgers, rare. 1 Shrimp Louie, dressing on the side."

> "Yes, Chef."

> "Yes, Chef."

The 2 stations responsible for the order reply.

As tickets arrive, aromas sweep through the kitchen in waves. Very distinct, wondrous smells, one after another; meat charring on grills, burgers on the flat top, onions sautéing. At the start of service, the waves are clear, defined.

As service goes on, aromas become mixed. They meld into a huge wave along with the clash of pans, heat of the grills, the sweat of the workers and behind it all, tension, like a big bass drum. Make it good; make it fast!

The Chef/Owner comes in after lunch service, the Sous Chef handles lunch.

In his 50's, Chef has jet black hair that he secretly dyes, but everybody knows better. A sometimes mustache (also dyed) that sometimes transforms into a 'soul tag' but never a beard. Overly long sideburns and a ponytail best not described. He has a middle-age male physique, big gut, little butt. Needs to lose 20 pounds, soon to be 30.

Chef graduated from the Culinary Institute of America in New York. In the *"same class as Bobby Flay,"* something he mentions at the drop of a Toque Blanche. He has cooked in big-time downtown restaurants in NYC and Chicago. What he is doing in Astoria, Oregon, is a little known, much discussed topic.

He has hinted at the Witness Protection Program;

> "I got cross-wise with the Mob and turned State's Evidence."

There are other stories but the most widely believed is the chef's ego, drinking and drug use got him fired from several high-profile New York restaurants. From NYC, he moved to Chicago where similar behavior made him leave town under a growing cloud. He worked in Portland for a short stretch and like so many other things that float down the Columbia River, Chef ended up in Astoria.

Dinner service is much longer, more intense than lunch. The lunch staff has left, replaced by the dinner crew. Dinner service is more of a marathon than a sprint; made worse by Chef. In the trade, he is known as a screamer. Standing at the pass-through, he examines each plate, making sure staff has properly executed the dish he created. If the plate doesn't meet his approval, reaction is immediate; lewd, crude and loud.

If the plate is exactly to his liking, Chef sends it out without comment.

At dinner, the kitchen has a different feel and smell. Aromas are fuller, richer. Sauces simmering, dinner rolls in the oven, chocolate melting, prime rib roasting.

As the food products prepared in advance run-out, they are quickly replaced by the kitchen prep crew.

> "Keep ahead, dammit! Keep ahead. We are not going in the weeds today."

This is Chef at the top of his substantial lungs. 'In the weeds' is a golf expression. A golfer who misses the fairway is in the rough or 'in the weeds.' In a restaurant kitchen, 'in the weeds' means getting behind on orders, usually from a lack of prepped ingredients.

Chef hates getting 'in the weeds' and you don't want to be the one who put him there.

Prepping food takes a lot of skill and practice. Watching someone with great 'knife skills' is like watching a really good pool player run the table. To prepare something as simple as carrots takes a good bit of skill. First, the peeled carrot is cut into a long rectangle, then into planks, then into smaller planks and finally sliced across the planks into perfectly shaped, miniature cubes. The carrot is transformed from a rugged, wrinkled vegetable into a golden-orange heap of tiny jewels. All in about 45 seconds.

The start of good knife skills is to prepare a hundred carrots every day. Every day for a couple of years.

At night, the kitchen is its own world. Noisy, stifling, crowded, but oddly comforting to those who have the skills, confidence and perseverance to be included in the exclusive club of the kitchen.

During a rare lull in dinner service, Chef heads out the back door for a smoke. He brings along his coffee cup; the cup is half full of vodka, no coffee. After the blast of nicotine and alcohol, Chef heads back into the kitchen. He is headed for the walk-in cooler to check on rib-eye inventory in the Steak Locker. The door to the Steak Locker is open. He slams the heavy door shut and marches back through the cooler screaming at the top of his voice,

> "Goddammit, I've told you all a million times, no one goes into the Steak Locker. My Locker, my steaks. I'm sick of you stealing from me. Only me , Charlie and the damn bookkeeper Marty, can go in there, period! All the rest of you losers stay the hell out."

Work in the kitchen stops. There is complete silence for a second, another second and then the kitchen starts again. Chef's wild rampage is not an isolated event.

Chef has some anger issues and a drinking problem. And several women issues, at least 3 of them. The blond waitress he's sleeping with now and the raven-haired cocktail waitress he dropped for the blond. And of course, the City Councilman's wife. The Councilman was an early investor in Steak Deluxe! He and his wife are one of Steak Deluxe!'s best customers and supporters. The wife more than the Councilman.

2

THE CHEF CAME TO ASTORIA as part of Pan-Asian Properties sweeping investment in Astoria. Pan-Asian's stated goal was to establish an ultra-high-end Resort.

The Resort would include an 18 story, 5-star hotel, along the Columbia River, with a marina dredged to berth the biggest mega-yachts. A heliport landing area adjacent to the hotel and a Jack Nicklaus designed golf course next to (and encroaching upon) Fort Clatsop National Park. And of course, the most expensive, biggest, most opulent Steak House in the West. That's where Chef came in. The perfect set-up for his ultimate come back!

The hotel (twice as tall as any other Astoria building and higher than the city's landmark, Astoria Column); the marina; heliport and Steak Deluxe!, were all to be located mostly on Clatsop County Port owned land, east of the Astoria-Megler Bridge. Steak Deluxe! was the only part of Pan-Asian's plan built.

There were initial hurdles. Pan-Asian was a lot less Asian than first thought and a lot more Russian. The face of the company consisted of a shady group of lawyers and financiers based in New York, with offshore contingents in Ukraine, Moscow and Monte Carlo. Cash was never part of the problem. Just the opposite, the project brought a flood of money to Astoria.

Pan-Asian rented an entire hotel for a month, leased a dozen vehicles from the Chevrolet dealer and filled a long-vacant downtown office building with furniture but hardly any employees. In addition, Pan-Asian opened accounts in almost every bank in Astoria.

From a big splash in the beginning, things turned suddenly south for Pan-Asian. 3 lawyers in New York were brought up on charges of lobbying for a foreign country (Ukraine) without State Department license.

Followed by a couple of financial officers indicted for fraud.

Also, logistical problems; the golf course, on land unsuited for golf. The property underwater for most of the winter. And the check to secure Jack Nicklaus's services bounced. The Port didn't have ownership of all the land needed for the Resort and would have to pursue Eminent Domain to get it. And for good measure, the Oregon State Lands Division had concerns about the marina. Oregon State doesn't own the water in the Columbia River, but it does own the riverbed.

And then locals. Not everybody in Astoria hated the planned Resort. The Chevy dealer thought it a good idea, as did a City Councilman. But that was about it. Too big, too out-of-place, too commercial and too damn NEW YORK CITY! Astorians believed their town to be more of a 'bed & breakfast' locale. Historical and scenic, perched on high hills overlooking the Columbia River, a walk-able, live-able small coastal town. The Resort didn't fit in with any of that.

When Pan-Asian collapsed, Chef cobbled together a group of investors and along with his own money, bought Steak Deluxe! at a fire-sale price. Keeping the ever-changing investor group in line is a full-time juggling act for the Chef.

3

THE MANAGER AT STEAK DELUXE! walks through the entire restaurant several times during dinner service. He wants a sense of how the whole operation is doing.

Charlie stops first at the reception counter.

> "How's it going, Cassi?"

> "So far, so good. No cancels. All reservations showed on time. Wait time on walk-ins is 40

minutes and we have been holding steady on that."

"Sounds good. Thanks"

"Charlie, when are we getting that new reservation software program?"

"Not now, Cassi. We'll talk about it tomorrow."

"That's what you said last week."

But Charlie is gone, on his way to the bar.

The bar is crowded and noisy but not loud, carpeting and plush upholstery took care of that. 12 patrons sat at the bar and another 15 at high top tables. 2 bartenders at each end of the bar, one is the bartender/manager, Bernie. The bar-back stands at the glassware washer, working like mad to keep up with incoming and outgoing drink glasses.

"Bernie, how's it going?"

"Good. Wait time is perfect for 1 drink, maybe 2. Stopped serving food at the bar top an hour ago, drinkers only at the bar now."

"Great, keep at it."

"Will do, Charlie."

Bernie is a restaurant/bar lifer, been at it since he was 18. Now in his early 30's, Bernie is proud to wear the same size 34 waist pants he wore in high school. He manages this by cinching up his belt <u>reeeeeal</u> tight under his ever-expanding belly. Bernie's trouser size has remained the same, but his shirts went from Medium to XXXLarge.

During busy services, bartenders are the production team for all drinks in the bar and dining room. They work in a tightly choreographed routine and rarely have time to look up to see who needs a drink at the bar. That's the bar-backs job. When a customer's glass is anywhere near empty, the bar-back lets the bartender know.

Drinkers at the high-top tables are the cocktail waitress's job.

"Bar-back, keep your eyes up," Charlie says on the way out.

"Yes, sir."

The bar-back is too new to be called by name.

Dinner service slowed down and the Chef removed his Toque and changed into a clean chef's jacket. The coffee cup he kept at the pass station had been refreshed with vodka several times. Through the swinging double-doors from the dining room come one of Astoria's most prominent couples, a City Councilman and his beautiful wife, Missy.

It is a weekly appearance by the Councilman and wife. They make a grand entrance at Steak Deluxe! and parade through the dining room. Shaking hands with people they know and waving at ones they don't, as if they had been childhood friends. Then on to the bar and a similar but shorter parade.

Next the kitchen, less handshaking and smiles here. Most kitchen workers are non-voters; this is a stop to see the Chef. The Councilman is a minority owner of Steak Deluxe! but acts if he held a majority share. Usually, the purpose of this stop is to grab a couple of free steaks to take home or cadge a couple of drinks.

This was the manager Charlie's complaint.

> "Dammit Chef, there's no way in hell the Steak Locker inventory will balance if you give away steaks every time the Councilman saunters in. And have you looked at his bar tab?"

The Chef's answer, always the same, a shrug of shoulders and no reply.

Handsome and smooth, always on the make and mostly on the take, the Councilman looks like he could be Tom Cruise's older brother. A brother that, like Tom, has looks for the movies, but this brother went into politics instead. Mid-60's but looks and acts younger. A lawyer who became a State Senator, ran for Governor twice, once as a Republican, once as a Democrat; lost both times.

The Councilman and his wife retired to Astoria and he ran successfully for City Council, currently serving his 4th term. He asks everyone to refer to him as 'Senator.'

He knows a lot of people but doesn't have any friends.

> "Look who's here, Missy, the Chef! Glad we caught you, always great to see you and the staff that makes this the best restaurant in Oregon."

The Councilman makes this pronouncement in a booming voice, turning 180 degrees so everyone could see and hear him. Missy, at her husband's side, made the same semi-circle, smiling and clapping her hands.

> "So nice of you two to stop in."

Chef can be an ass with staff but can turn on charm for customers and investors. He's ready to hit up the Councilman for a cash infusion.

Missy turned her dazzling smile on the Chef,

> "We need to discuss the menu for the Senator's Re-election Kickoff dinner."

> "We are honored to hold the dinner at Steak Deluxe!, Missy. Let me get my notes and we can meet in the bar."

There is a empty high-top table in the bar. Missy dislikes high tables; a petite woman, she hates having to hoist herself into the tall chairs, no place to put her feet, legs swinging free like a small child on a church pew.

She would talk to Chef about it later. The next meeting would be in the dining room or someplace more private. And without her husband.

Missy is an attractive lady of a 'certain age.' probably mid to late '50s, but Botox, a personal trainer and a huge Nordstrom bill, make her look 10 years younger. Blond hair, blue eyes, stunning figure.

She and her husband have a pact; in public, they have a united, well-married front. In private, their driven natures are directed to their own singular goals & desires.

"So, here's a rough sketch of your Kick-Off Dinner; Steak Deluxe! will close that night from 5pm until 8pm. All previous reservations have been moved to later that night or another date."

"The Senator and I appreciate that, Chef. We hope to be able to show our thanks in some way." Missy said the last part with a small smile and a wink her husband did not see.

"Here's what we'll do," Chef began, "appetizers; grilled shrimp wrapped with prosciutto, deviled eggs with caviar and artichoke hearts stuffed with crab. These will be served with Champagne by passing waiters. We'll start at 5 in the main dining room. At the same time, no-host cocktails in the bar for those who want hard liquor and are willing to pay for it."

"It sounds wonderful, Chef."

"Thanks. It will be. At 6 everybody gets seated and dinner service starts. 1st course; beet and blue cheese salad on baby arugula, with balsamic dressing and baguettes from Blue Scorcher Bakery. We'll pair that with Pinot Gris from Terra Vina.

Entrée choices are Filet Mignon with demi-glace or Salmon with apricot/ginger sauce; both served with roasted new potatoes, chives and Asiago tuile. The guests can choose 2017 Ribbon Springs Chardonnay from Adelsheim or 2016 'Dundee Hills' Pinot Noir from De Ponte, depending on their entrée."

"Wow!" Missy was excited, her husband, nodding and smiling but not listening.

> "Chef, Missy, you 2 know this stuff. Hell, I'd just as soon have clam strips and beer. Let me just chat a bit with the guys in the kitchen. They work so hard and never get enough credit."

> "OK," the Chef and Missy said it in unison.

The Councilman kissed his wife on the cheek and left after an awkward fist bump with the Chef.

With the Councilman gone, things moved faster.

> "By 7, we'll have all tables cleared. Then we serve sorbet and more Champagne. Everybody will think its dessert, so after the money pitch and speech, the real desert will be a surprise."

> "Perfect," Missy practically purred.

> "We'll keep Champagne flowing through the donations. If you want good pledges, you got to get them liquored up. Next is the Senator's speech; after that, we roll out his birthday cake."

> "He makes such a big damn deal about his birthday. It's like I married an 8-year-old child."

The Chef continued.

> "After he blows out candles on his cake, everybody gets a miniature cake with a lit candle." It was one of Steak Deluxe!'s signature items. "The big donors get Spanish coffee, tableside. The whole deal; sky-high brandy pour, flambé, big production. I'm bringing a couple of guys down from Huber's in Portland to handle it.
>
> "At 7:45, we get everybody out. I need to get the room cleaned and set up so I can salvage some money out of the night. I'm getting killed on this."

Chef had a profit problem with this event and needed to bring it up.

> "We agreed on the price a long time ago, Chef. If it doesn't work for you, I've got another restaurant dying for the chance. I know the Chef there too."

She smiled, one eyebrow raised, and Chef knew he had lost.

When the Councilman got to the kitchen, staff had already left. Maylen, the Pastry Chef, was at her station by herself.

"Maylen, you look hotter every time I see you."

"Hello, Councilman." The reply is soft, dismissive. This was not their first encounter.

"Darling, call me Senator, you know a 2 term Senator, re-elected in a gr__"

"I know you told me." *Several times.*

"Honey, come on, treat me right. We need to get together . . . maybe drinks, a late dinner?"

"The only thing we needed to 'get together' on is desserts for the kick-off dinner and I've done that with your wife."

"Now come on, I'm talking about you & me not th__"

"I do need to talk to your wife again."

"About the event? That's all settled." The 'Senator' was getting a bit flustered.

"No, not the event. I need to talk to your wife about her low-life, totally disgusting husband."

"Now listen, darling__"

"No. You listen. Leave now & don't ever come back." Again, the voice soft but very firm.

4

THE DINING ROOM IS REFERRED to as *front of house* in the restaurant trade. The bar, which is usually near the front of a restaurant, is called the bar. The kitchen is always called the kitchen.

Tonight, front of house staff at Steak Deluxe! are slammed. Every table full, reception area packed, a line of eager diners stretching out the door.

The kitchen and its staff are also slammed. Just like front of house. Just as crazy, just as many balls in the air. But front of house is different. In front, they don't see you sweat. In the kitchen, a line cook is probably sweating into the béarnaise sauce.

In front of house, the tension is sky-high but tightly held. Like a play that for any number of reasons could fall apart mid-performance, front of house staff, actors all, hold everything together. Barely.

> "Table 3 is getting mutinous. They've been here almost an hour. No food. The guy that ordered steak has the knife in his hand. He keeps waving it at me".

> "If he stabs you, let me know. Until then, comp drinks for the table."

> "Did that, half an hour ago."

> "Do it again!"

> "If I get stabbed, I'm quitting."

The waitress is complaining to the manager, Charlie, like he doesn't have enough of his own problems. A faded TV star with his 2 decades younger date is standing in front of him, demanding to be seated immediately.

> "I want a table NOW; you know who I am."

And that sealed it for Charlie. The jackass would never be seated, not tonight, not any night.

"Sir, the first table that opens is yours. But for now, please step outside. At the end of the line. Thank you."

Charlie was good at his job but terrible with his life. Bankrupt twice, married 3 times. And the 3rd marriage is about to end; he just doesn't know when. Charlie has been through it all before; he knows the signs and, for some reason, just can't get out of the way of the oncoming train wreck.

In addition to the professional problems of managing a high-end, high drama restaurant, Charlie has personal issues. The raven-haired waitress, Rachel? The one Chef dumped? Charlie had been dating her but didn't know Chef was too; at the same time!

Charlie once had thoughts about leaving his wife for Rachel.

Charlie, 45 years old, two-timed by a 23-year-old and he hadn't had a clue. And now what, take her back and have it happen again? He did have to admit to a bit of two-timing on his part. With the big, blond waitress. Nothing serious yet, but maybe.

And of course, there was his wife.

And financial issues. Mortgaged and leveraged right up to his red-tinged blue eyes. Charlie was promised a big bonus, one that could get him above water for the first time in years. No one thought he could achieve it. Charlie achieved it and more. Highest gross ever, highest profit ever.

Chef and his investor group said they couldn't afford to pay him the bonus.

"We never thought you'd make it."

The bonus was a bright light of hope for Charlie and it looked like it had burned out.

The night wore on. 2 specials sold out, then the rib-eyes and tri-tip sold out as well. Luckily, the Steak Deluxe! Burger lasted through service. If it sold out, there could have been a riot.

The kitchen closed at 10:30pm, the last diners left 11pm and the bar shut down at midnight. Everybody bone-tired; front of house, bar and kitchen. Everybody.

Bone-tired but also jubilant, they'd pulled it off. Again.

Big tips in front of house and bar; straight hourly wage in the kitchen. It isn't right, but it's what it is. Chef gave a case of beer to the kitchen crew; it didn't make it right, but it helped. A little.

Kitchen crew left the minute the beer was gone. Front of house staff left after everyone tipped out. Waiters tipped runners, busboys and bartenders; cocktail waitresses tipped bartenders and bartenders tipped the bar-back.

Charlie, Chef and Bernie, the bar manager, stayed behind, had a celebratory drink at the bar. Actually, more than one.

> "Before I forget Chef, we had another problem with the Councilman. He was hitting on a woman at the bar, good looking redhead. Her husband was pissed and the woman looked like she was gonna clock the Councilman with her purse. Everybody at the bar saw it."
>
> "Damn that prick." Bernie had told the Chef similar stories in the past.
>
> "I told him he was wanted at the reception desk, he got up and I moved the redhead and her husband into the dining room. They were having the drink at the bar, waiting for a table. It was their anniversary." Bernie stopped talking long enough to fix himself another drink. "It could of ruined their evening but I comped them a couple of French 75's and it seemed to calm them down. I think Shelly comped them desert as well."

Charlie weighed in;

"For those of us keeping score; comped drinks and dessert, there's $50 right there. Plus, that couple will tell all their friends about the weird evening at our restaurant. None of it our fault but we take the blame and the cost."

"We got to do something about that guy." Bernie again.

"Hard to do much, I need his money. Pure and simple, I need his money. Thanks for telling me. Thanks guys, good work."

The Chef shook hands with each man and headed out the door, Bernie right behind him.

Charlie finished his duties, turned out lights and left the restaurant at 1:30am.

Long after everyone else had gone home.

5

STEAK DELUXE! WAS MEANT to be a 'Statement Structure.' And it is. The statement made is class and opulence; 2 details that rarely come together. At Steak Deluxe! class and opulence met and melded.

Set on a prime chunk of Astoria's waterfront, the restaurant is a large rectangle. Facing North, the long side of the rectangle gives diners a spectacular view of the Riverwalk and Columbia River, through its massive 30-foot high windows. The outdoor deck is a prized spot for both Bar and Dining Room customers during summer months.

Facing West, the short side of the rectangle, the Bar at Steak Deluxe! has a beautiful view of the Astoria-Megler Bridge, towering 200 feet over the Columbia River and gracefully descending to a 3-mile causeway to the Washington State side of the River.

After leaving their car keys with the valet, a guest approaching Steak Deluxe! see's a formidable, even intimidating building. The entrance is on the South facing, long side of the rectangle. It shows an elegant V-shape roofline. At both ends, the V is 38-feet tall, tapering to 25-feet in the middle of the roof. The 2 sides of the V meet at a large skylight that runs above the center of the restaurant.

The front door of Steak Deluxe! is massive. 18 feet tall, 8 feet wide, painted a brilliant red . . . the door doesn't open. After trying both massive brass doorknobs and knocking uncertainly on the door itself, guests notice 2 smaller glass doors, sitting on either side of the red door. They automatically open.

Customers change from irritated, to surprised, then embarrassed and finally initiated into a secretive club. When they bring first-timers to Steak Deluxe! they stand back, watching with a smug smile, as their friends struggle at the door.

The architect stole the idea from Per Se New York.

On both sides of the entrance doors, there is a 10-feet high expanse of frosted glass running to the sides of the building. This frosted glass adds to the exclusive feeling; shapes moving, filtered candlelight, an enclave that can't be clearly seen, but one that creates an urgency to enter.

Above the frosted glass is clear glass all the way to the roof. This allows natural light to flood the restaurant.

Beyond the front doors, both real and false, is the Reception area. Beautiful rugs, tasteful furnishings, all understated and according to the Manager too damn big.

> "Chef, we need to cut Reception back. Let more people wait in the Bar; make some income off their wait".

The Chef/Owner, instrumental in the design of Steak Deluxe!, is not interested in employee critiques.

> "Thank you for your input, Charlie. Anything else? No? Great. Back to work."

To the right of Reception is the Kitchen. It is hidden, not to be seen by the public.

The Chef said,

"Open kitchen, my ass! I want a closed kitchen. Don't want people seeing what we do 'under the hood' in here."

To the left of Reception is the Bar, with its stage and dance floor. Looking left, a knock-out view of the Bridge, facing forward, an equally impressive view of the River. The actual bar itself is massive, 20 feet long, 25 feet tall, with a beautiful display of bottles and glassware. It is the dividing point between the Bar and Dining Room.

Protocol for *'monetizing'* guests begins early at Steak Deluxe! Most diners stop at the Bar first, whether they want to or not. There is always a delay in getting seated for dinner at Steak Deluxe!

"We are making sure your table is ready. Please wait in the Bar and I'll be right back to you."

This is said by a handsome host or hostess, in a comforting voice. In the restaurant business, it's called a *soft command.* The intention is to have you sit at the Bar, spend 20 to 30 of your dollars, then we'll be back to seat you. It almost always works.

If it doesn't work, diners are escorted directly through the rear of Reception into the Dining Room.

Spacious and elegant; the Dining Room has soft lighting, beautiful floral displays, flowers at every table. The tables lavishly set and the chairs wildly comfortable ($700 each). All of this designed to promote a luxurious experience that will encourage large amounts of money to pass from diner's wallets to Steak Deluxe!

Class and opulence at Steak Deluxe! came at a cost, a considerable cost. It was one of the many factors in the failure of Pan-Asian Inc.

6

CHARLIE FELL ASLEEP in his recliner, with a half-empty beer in one hand, remote in the other, watching a black & white re-run of *Gunsmoke*. He woke up at 8am when he spilled beer over his lap and most of the recliner.

Charlie's wife already had left for work. She and Charlie hardly ever spoke anymore. It reminded Charlie of an old joke;

When you first get married, there's 'everywhere sex'. On the floor, the kitchen table, in the shower. As the marriage matures, it's 'missionary sex, in the bedroom, missionary position. After that 'hallway sex'. That's where spouses pass in the hallway and one says to the other, "Screw You!"

Charlie left for work at 8:45am in his aging Ford Taurus. He lives in Warrenton; his commute is 8 minutes. When Charlie lived and worked in Portland, there was a commute of 20 miles, 45 minutes each way. His commute now isn't bad, but today he hated it. Hated his car, hated his job, hated his entire life and everything in it.

Well, not everything. He didn't hate his wife, he felt sorry for her. And he felt immensely sorry and sad for himself. Tomorrow is Valentine's Day, the biggest volume day at any restaurant. All hands-on deck. Balls to the wall busy. Lots of business, big tips. Charlie wasn't ready for any of it. Mentally, physically and in every other possible way, Charlie was down, almost out.

At Steak Deluxe!, Charlie is a positive leader and a terrible delegator. Every problem seems to land on Charlie. He hates his job and his job is his life.

Right then, he remembered the TV interview. Channel 8 from Portland tomorrow at noon. The 'Ultimate Restaurant' in Oregon for the 'Ultimate Valentine's Day Date.' All of it, Chef's doing. The perfect outlet for his all-encompassing ego. One more damn thing on th_

Charlie managed to hit his brakes before he rear-ended the Mercedes in front of him.

When he got to the restaurant, in his small, cluttered office, Charlie saw a scrawled note from Marty, the bookkeeper.

CHARLIE, THE ON HAND FOR STEAKS IN THE LOCKER IS OFF, <u>AGAIN</u>!!!

BEGINNING INVENTORY – SALES – PURCHASES – ON HAND INVENTORY

DON'T MATCH UP!!!

ON HAND <u>WAY</u> TOO SMALL

One more damn problem that became Charlie's damn problem. Should have been Chef's, but no, Charlie would have to fix it. In the worst funk of his adult life, Charlie went to the kitchen, opened the walk-in cooler door, went through to the Steak Locker. He punched in his code on the wall-mounted keypad, pressed Enter and opened the heavy door.

That's when a body fell out of the Steak Locker on to the cooler's cement floor.

Cold, blue, dead.

Charlie isn't sure what he is seeing. He backs out of the cooler, goes back in. Yep, that's right; it is what he's seeing. The Councilman . . . . dead; a knife, one of the knives from the Wagyu Burger, sticking out of his chest.

For reasons he could never explain, even to himself, Charlie goes to the body, pulls the knife out, getting blood on his hands, pants, shoes and floor.

The body is the former State Senator, now Astoria City Councilman. Smooth, corrupt, constantly on the make. Now, deader than a doornail.

To make a dumb move dumber, Charlie gets behind the Councilman, grabs him under his arms, hauls him back into the Steak Locker.

He drags the Councilman to a far corner and leaves him. The body sitting upright on the floor, legs sticking straight out.

Shit, shit . . . that won't work! Charlie runs around the Locker like a pinball, looking for something to cover the body, some way to hide it. He finally spots an apron and empty potato sack. *Neither of which should be in here, dammit!* In a fever pitch, Charlie takes all the steaks off one section of shelving. He moves the shelves out enough to get the body behind them and lays it flat. The apron and sack cover the Councilman's body. Charlie shoves the shelves back into position. The sound of the shelves jamming the corpse against the wall makes Charlie want to vomit.

Charlie throws steaks back on the shelves; he is done.

Steak Locker door shut, lock reset. As he stumbles through the cooler, Charlie almost steps on the bloody knife; he grabs it and notices blood on the floor. Not a lot, but enough for him to walk through it. Almost out of his mind, Charlie can only come up with taking off his shoes and throwing 3 bags of potatoes over the bloody mess. He knows it's only a temporary fix, but it's all he has.

Holding his shoes, Charlie lets himself out of the cooler, closes the door. He stands, with his back against the door, leaning hard, ready to fall down.

His life, not all that great to begin with, has turned suddenly, completely, to shit.

It was a slow day for both lunch and dinner. Charlie moved enough products out of the Steak Locker, into the cooler to cover both services. He made up a story about a mechanical problem in the Locker and a repairman coming from Portland tomorrow. The Chef had the day off.

Charlie couldn't come to grips with the hard fact there is a dead guy in the Steak Locker and he has to do something about it!

Jim Hallaux

Through all of this, there is a soft voice in his head, that Charlie can't seem to hear,

Charlie, Charlie, why are you covering up something you didn't do?

7

CHARLIE COULDN'T SLEEP THAT NIGHT. All he can think about is the dead guy, the knife, the blood. Finally, he gives up. Gets dressed, goes to Pig & Pancake. Sits at the counter, 6am, he's the only customer. Charlie orders breakfast. As he waits, he thinks about the cooler they must have at the Pig. For the millionth time, Charlie considers the nightmare waiting for him in the Locker at Steak Deluxe.

Breakfast arrives, Charlie can't eat it. Couldn't sleep and now can't eat.

He puts $30 on the counter and leaves. Like all restaurant people, Charlie is a big tipper.

Back at Steak Deluxe! Charlie sits at his desk for an hour, not moving. Not trying to control thoughts whirling through his head. He can't control anything; his mind, his job, the dead guy in the Locker; none of it.

Suddenly it comes to him; *I'll go to the police.* I haven't done anything wrong. *Didn't kill anybody. Did act stupidly, but if stupid was criminal, everybody'd be in jail. Shouldn't have moved the body, shouldn't have pulled the knife out, . . .jeesus shouldn't have the damn knife in my desk drawer right now!*

Getting the knife out of the drawer reminded him of the mess in the Steak Locker. Even though he had decided to call the police, he goes down to the Locker, for no other reason than putting off the inevitable.

Charlie opens the cooler and walks in. The potatoes sacks left on the floor are gone, no bloodstains. *Did I dream that?* Charlie punches in his code, opens the Steak Locker door. He walks trance-like to the corner of the Locker and moves the shelves.

No body.

8

VALENTINE'S DAY.

Chef speaking to the assembled staff:

> "This TV interview is the most important thing
> that has happened to me in Astoria. After it
> airs, this restaurant will be packed; I will be
> under a lot of scrutiny. Bigger crowds, more
> problems and more critics. I must be at my
> best, how you perform your jobs will reflect on

me . . . . and the restaurant. Let's not screw this up".

It was the best the Chef could do. All about him, all the time, but here he managed to mention there were other people involved.

The day's deliveries started, 1st the florist, 150 roses. All women patrons would get a rose at dinner service. Seafood deliveries came next; Salmon from Ocean Beauty arrived first, next oysters from Ekone Oyster Company in Bay Center, Washington. A busboy got the honor of driving Chef's Eldorado pickup across the River and up the North side of Willapa Bay to get them.

If you're an oyster lover, chances are you've had a Willapa Bay oyster. 1 in every 4 oysters consumed in the US comes from pristine Willapa Bay. Willapa Bay is a shallow inland sea 25 miles long, 8 miles wide. At low tide ½ of the water is gone from the Bay. This twice-daily replenishment of saltwater and remote location makes Willapa Bay the cleanest estuary in the nation.

Classic Willapa Bay flavor is lightly salty, sweetly cucumber, as pure sea as you can get in an oyster.

Kitchen staff had spent the last 2 days cutting sides of beef into entrees. Filled to almost over-flowing, the Steak Locker had 350 servings of meat ready to go. Tonight, every table will order at least one steak entrée.

Pastry Chef Maylen made 200 Chocolate Kahlua Tarts the day before. Tarts consist of a walnut crust, filled with a chocolate espresso/liqueur filling, topped with crystallized ginger crema. It is a recipe a home baker could make if they had a decade of experience making commercial desserts. This is the biggest project of the year for Maylen. It took 2 weeks of planning and 18 hours of labor to make the tarts perfect. They rest on a shelf in the cooler with a hand-lettered sign; DISTURB THESE & DIE.

Tall and slender, with long shiny black hair, Maylen is extremely quiet but not shy. She has a slightly Asian look to her face, especially her eyes. Maylen fits the stereotype of a Pastry Chef, part of the kitchen staff, but at the same time separate from it. Like the place kicker on a football team.

Maylen is a quiet person, a good listener. To kitchen staff, she is the go-to for personal problems, although they do call her 'Ice Queen' behind her back.

Front of house staff found her helpful but reserved, a bit standoff-ish. Asked several times to join waitresses for an after-shift drink, Maylen graciously declines.

She does speak with servers after each service to make sure there were no pastry complaints. Maylen asks for suggestions and often incorporates them into her baking.

Maylen is comfortable talking, learning and listening to both kitchen and wait staff.

The crew from Channel 8 TV showed up early, at 9:30am. Chef couldn't believe all the people, equipment and lights this interview required. He had written out a script and read it to the reporter and producer of the segment. They listened politely, the producer said;

> "That's great Chef, thanks. Jennifer here will ask the questions; it's a 2-shot set-up, so when you answer, look at her, not the camera. Don't worry if you slip up; we will edit any problems."

After a bit of make-up for the reporter and a lot for the Chef, the interview started; first in the dining room, then bar, kitchen and finally the Steak Locker.

Each new area required set-up and break-down for the TV crew. All of this took time, a lot of time. Start to finish, the interview process took 2 hours. All this effort for 6 minutes of airtime.

Charlie was a wreck through all of this. He moved tables and chairs in the dining room to get the right

camera angle for the TV crew. After they were done, he moved chairs back, then re-set tables. Same procedure in the bar; similar thing in the kitchen. He did all this in a dark cloud that swirled around him and seemed to invade his mind.

The Steak Locker was the worst. Charlie kept looking at the floor, expecting to see blood. Chef raved on endlessly about his *'Cathedral of Meat'* (Channel 8 edited this down to a reasonable length). Standing just inside of the Locker, Charlie held on to a shelf to remain standing. He watched Chef's performance but didn't listen to it. He knew if he concentrated too closely, he would see the Councilman's image wedged between the shelves and the wall.

The Steak Locker segment finally done, Chef saw Charlie clinging to a shelf, white as a sheet.

> "Jeesus, Charlie, are you OK? You look like a ghost."

Charlie didn't care what he looked like; he just didn't want to see the bloodstained ghost of the Councilman rise-up in the Steak Locker.

Chef had offered lunch to the gang from Channel 8, he hoped for some private time with the reporter, but it didn't work out. She and her crew had a 2-hour drive back to Portland to edit footage and get the piece cleared for air during the 6pm news hour.

Lunch service was slow, as always on Valentine's Day. Everybody was saving their stomachs and wallets for dinner.

Senior citizens comprised the first dinner seating at 4:30pm. As the evening went on, patron's age level went down. Working couples (who could find a sitter) showed up between 5:30 and 6:30. Between 7 and 8, people who'd made reservations months in advance. At 9, true romantics; cocktails first, appetizers, (oysters for the gentleman, crab for the lady) Champagne or Chardonnay to start, salads, entrées (usually steak for both), a bottle of Pinot Noir and finally a Chocolate Kahlua Tart or some other glorious dessert, with Baileys and coffee. $300 to $350, not counting tip, add another $75 for that. After 10pm, it was diners who couldn't get in anywhere else sooner.

Charlie arrived at the restaurant at 8am and worked until the last guest left. Didn't take a break, didn't stop for lunch. On the move constantly, he was everywhere; dining room, kitchen, bar. Charlie's body moved, but his mind was frozen.

"Charlie, snap out of it. You've been standing in front of the desk for the last 5 minutes; people are trying to get in." That's about as angry as Cassi got.

"Sorry," Charlie mumbled as he moved on to the bar.

"What do you want, Charlie?"

"Sorry Bernie, I can't remember why I came in here."

"Well, get out and maybe you'll remember. But move; I'm trying to make drinks for about 100 thirsty people. Bring ice when you come back."

Charlie left but forgot to bring the ice.

At midnight it was over. There were still a few customers in the bar, but the Chef moved them out with a loud shout:

"OK kids, thanks for coming in, now it's time to leave. Drink up and get out."

His next move, even more remarkable;

"Charlie, get the guys from the kitchen up here, drag Maylen along with them."

The assembled staff numbered about 30; some thought they were getting fired. Others thought the restaurant must be closing. Everybody was wrong.

> "Thank you for your hard work today. You made me proud. Drinks are on the house."

It was the busiest Bernie and the other bartender had been all night and it had been a remarkably busy night. Employees who normally drank Smirnoff vodka, ordered Grey Goose. Those who drank Scoresby scotch switched to Johnnie Walker Black. Bourbon drinkers moved up to Pendleton and Crown Royal. Kitchen staff moved from Bud Light to Bud Light and a shot of Patron.

Charlie, his pay based on net profit, said;

> "Chef, I'm not sure this is a good idea."

He said this as he ordered another double Crown Royal on the rocks.

It was the first-time management and staff of Steak Deluxe! felt they were all part of the same team.

Charlie, again, the last to leave. He turned off lights in the restaurant, a job that took a good 20 minutes. Finally, as he got to the front door, Charlie remembered he hadn't bought his wife a Valentine's Day present.

He went back into the restaurant and made his way to the kitchen. There were a couple of cannoli's left at the Pastry station. Charlie left the kitchen after turning off two more lights the kitchen crew bastards had left on. On the way, in the dark, he hit his knee, HARD, on a low-boy refrigerator, dropping the pastries on the floor.

As Charlie walked to his car, he tried to dust the cannoli's off, his present to his wife of 7 years.

On Valentine's Day.

9

THE NIGHT BEFORE.

How did the body get moved? Well . . . . . it wasn't all that hard.

Ricardo, '*not Ricky dammit,*' was up for just about anything, so not a big surprise that he agreed to this undefined errand. The late-night timing did give him pause. But he went along.

After short stints at every other Astoria restaurant, Ricardo landed at Steak Deluxe! as a dishwasher.

Short, slight, with black eyes and hair, he had a winning smile that needed significant dental work. Ricardo spoke fast and way too often. This was due to a cocaine/meth/alcohol habit he'd picked up early in life. This explained his spotty work history.

Tonight, Ricardo came back to Steak Deluxe! as requested at 3am. Stood for 10 minutes in the dark waiting, smoking. Then the kitchen door opened,

"Come on in; we have some work to do in the Steak Locker."

Ricardo knew the rules.

"Can I go in there?"

"It's OK this one time."

They went into the walk-in cooler, at the far end, the Steak Locker door stood wide open.

"Come in, over here, help me move this shelf."

"Good God, this guy's dead! He's dead!" Ricardo's scream came out hard & high.

"I know."

"I mean jeesus . . . . . dead . . . . real dead."

"I know."

"Who . . . who . . . who killed him"?

"Ricky, the less you know, the better off you are."

"What're we gonna do? What . . . What we gonna do? I'm getting paid, right?

"Yes, you are getting paid, all we have to do is a little clean-up, wrap the body in canvas and haul it out."

The body was wrapped, tied up tightly and lugged out the back door of the restaurant and piled into the back of a car.

Next and last stop was off Marine Drive, down from Steak Deluxe! on the bank of the Columbia River where 3 vacant warehouses stood. No wind, not much light, silent. The body drug out on an abandoned pier and, without ceremony, dropped off the end. The tide had turned, running to low, water flying by. Next stop for the Councilman; Yokohama.

"When do I get paid?"

"Right now." The long, slim knife went deep into Ricardo's heart. Killing him before he hit the water.

Ricardo's body followed the Councilman's downriver.

"Thanks for your help, Ricky."

10

"WHERE IN THE HELL IS RICKY? We got dishes stacked up to the ceiling in there."

Lunch service at Steak Deluxe is in full swing.

"This is the 2nd damn day. Call him at home, tell him if he's not here in 5 minutes, don't come in at all."

The Chef was in a foul mood to begin with; a no-show dishwasher didn't help.

"Donny, get in the dish pit. Start washing."

"You said I got promoted. I'm working the line today."

"And now I'm telling you to get in the dish pit or join your buddy Ricky on the unemployment line."

"Some damn promotion." Donny said the last part under his breath. He didn't want to argue, but he did want to plant a big ol' frying pan upside the Chef's head.

Lunch service ended, still no Ricky.

"Maybe he's at home doing Lucy."

That was the last word on Ricky. No one called him, stopped by his apartment or mentioned his name again. He was part of the kitchen team and then, he wasn't.

Mayen opened the door to the women's staff restroom and bumped into Missy, the Councilman's wife. There were few women on the kitchen staff; they didn't usually last long. Maylen got used to having the restroom to herself, her private sanctuary.

Missy stood in front of the sink, head down, hands spread wide on the counter. She was crying. Maylen looked at her; didn't say anything.

Missy lifted her head, saw Maylen and said;

"Men are shits. All of them."

Maylen agreed whole-heartedly but didn't reply.

"My sister sent me a book last year. *'Why Men Lie & Cheat.'* I didn't read it then; now I'll have to."

"Missy, I wouldn't have to read the book; I could write that book."

"Thanks, Maylen. Roger hasn't come home in 2 days. No phone call, no text. Nothing."

Roger? Maylen didn't recognize the 'Senator's' given name. When she thought of him, it wasn't by name, she thought of a jackass; a loud, braying, jackass.

"He's done this before, catting around. But always in Vegas or LA, not here in Astoria." Missy started crying again.

The conversation went on for another 20 minutes, Missy talking and crying; Maylen listening with an occasional comment.

"Thanks, Maylen; I can use a friend right about now."

"Let me know how I can help. I'm here for you."

"I'm sorry I did all of the talking about myself, Maylen. How are you doing? I never see you with anyone. Do you have a life outside Steak Deluxe!? Aren't you afraid you'll miss out?"

"I'm not loving anybody right now, Missy, and I'm not afraid of anything."

Charlie held an after-service briefing with all areas of the restaurant. No significant problems, just bitching. The Chef bitching about his kitchen crew, crew bitching about the Chef. All of them complaining about produce; winter in Oregon, what did they expect? Maylen, as usual, didn't have anything negative to say. She did mention a couple of things that could lower Pastry costs. Charlie said he'd follow through and he would.

Everything OK in the bar, Charlie moved on to the dining room. Runners whined about ticket times and the Chef's behavior at the pass-through. Waiters complained about the runners, the Chef and each other.

And Charlie wondered why his hair was thinning.

Last stop, the Reception Desk, Cassi handled Reception and all reservations. Her attitude; calm, cool and collected. It wasn't just her work attitude; it was who she was.

> "Hi Cassi, how's it going."
>
> "Things are good here, but you look a little down at the mouth. Everything OK?"
>
> "Everything is usual with me. Usual problems, usual bitching. And my continuing dislike for having to deal with adults who act like children."
>
> "Except for me, right Charlie?"
>
> "Yes, except for you."

Charlie had to admit she was right. He also had to admit; he hadn't thought much about her. He didn't have to; she did her job well, never a problem, everybody liked her. What was there to think about? Well . . . now that he paid attention to her, for what seemed like the first time, there was a lot to think about.

Starting with her eyes, sparkling, ocean-blue eyes, looking at Charlie right now in a way that made him a bit nervous. And her beautiful smile. Cassi is a living, breathing character from the 1950's TV show 'Ozzie & Harriet' transported to present day. She is the type of woman you bring home to meet Mom.

"Charlie, you're kind of zoning out on me."

"Sorry, I was, I . . . . was thinking about you."

"Well, dream on big boy." There, that smile again.

"I realized I haven't told you what a cheerful, outgoing, capable person you are, Cassi."

"Gees Charlie, you make me sound like your favorite aunt."

Charlie didn't have a come-back. For a guy who usually thought of most women with hidden but barely contained lust, he never had that with Cassi. Maybe it was her age, she seemed in her early 30's, but could be older. Maybe that was it; most of his dates and marriages were with younger women.

But something else struck Charlie. Maybe she seemed too good for him.

Cassi took a long look at Charlie. She notices his attention but has zero interest in returning it. The last thing she needs is to get wrapped up in a workplace romance with Charlie, a man who seems to have someone on the side. Cassi won't be that someone.

> "OK, enough dreaming on company time. Let's go over this week's reservations."

As he was leaving the restaurant, Charlie was served with divorce papers.

When he got home, his wife and all her things were gone.

No note.

11

CHARLIE CAUGHT CHEF DURING his mid-morning smoke break. He noticed the cigarette in the Chef's left hand and coffee cup in his right. No steam is rising from the coffee. But the hands were steadier than usual, a good sign. And Chef's face looked a lighter shade of grey today.

On a scale of 1 to 10, the Chef came in at a strong 4.7

"Hey Chef."

"Hey Charlie."

"The girl's group is leaving for Cabo next week."

"Damn, is it that time of year already? Again, with that trip?"

3 of the best servers at Steak Deluxe!, all women, went on a yearly week-long 'sabbatical' to Baja California. The restaurant took a hit while they were gone, slow turn-over of tables, less 'up-selling', more customer complaints.

"They're a pretty militant group Chef. You threatened to fire them if they left last year and they didn't sell a single dessert for the next 2 weeks. Remember? We had to back down."

"And when they came back, it took them almost a week to sober up."

'You're right. I'm surprised they're going back to Cabo. One of them got arrested last trip and had to pay a big bribe to get out."

"OK, OK, Charlie, we give in again. Who do you have as replacements?"

"Mickey Tagger and__"

"You mean Shaky? Last year he broke more than he sold."

"He is a little clumsy."

"He's an earthquake on 2 feet."

"The other one, Chef, is John Twist."

"Stink Twist? The one with a gas problem? That John?"

"He's on a new course of probiotics. Say's it helps."

"Just to be clear Charlie, all you could come up with is Shaky & Stinky."

"Yes."

"Maybe we should close for the week."

They didn't close. Sales and profits did take a dip. For the record, Shaky had a slim margin, on the plus side for sales vs. breakage. The probiotics John Twist took were a help but not a cure.

The girls showed up at Portway Tavern the night before they were due back at Steak Deluxe! They were still 3 beautiful women but looked a little worse for wear around the edges.

"Welcome back, ladies! Can I buy you a drink?"

"Thanks, Charlie. Just a Coke, I'm not drinking for a year."

"Me, either Charlie."

"The same for me, Charlie, I'm not drinking until tomorrow."

"How was your trip to Cabo?"

"Didn't go to Cabo. Flew into Cabo, then drove to Todos Santos."

"Got it. I always wanted to go there. How was it?"

"Fun, out of control. In the bars, we kept hearing about wild parties on the beach, with crazy women. Turns out the crazy women, they were us."

12

BOTH MEN ARE BIG.

Real big, twice the size of Marty, the bookkeeper. Both blond, crewcuts, blue eyes, massive biceps.

They stared at Marty.

"This guy's pikkuruinen." One of the giant's mumbles under his breath.

What language are they talking? Finnish? Swedish? Pretty sure Finnish. Marty swiftly became more concerned about their size than their ethnicity.

They barely fit in Marty's office. Walked in unannounced, like it was their office.

"How can I help you?"

"We're here to help you, Marty."

"Have we met before, I don-"

"We're meeting now, Marty. We're your new meat resource."

"What did you say?"

"I said, Marty, we are your new meat resource."

"All meat products at Steak Deluxe! are raised and fattened in Svenson, exclusively for us. They are processed in Clatsop Plains, we age and cut in-house. It's an exacting process that we developed. No one else does this."

"Great Marty, but we'll take care of all that now."

"But . . . but I . . . "

"You have plenty on your plate, hey that's kind
of funny, isn't it? On your plate – restaurant,
get it . . . . "

The 2 big guys chuckled. Marty stared at them, silent,
waiting for this weird episode to be over. *How in the
hell did they get in here?*

After several awkward minutes of silence, the bigger
of the 2 huge men, spoke up,

"Marty, we'll take care of it, we'll also make
sure nothing bad happens here."

"Bad happens? What are you talking about?"
Good God, these guys are enormous!

"Make sure nobody gets roughed up walking to
their car after work. Make sure the cars are
safe. Nobody slashes tires, bashes in windows.
That sort of thing won't happen."

"OK, OK."

Marty was getting flustered and worse; these guys
were scaring the shit out of him.

"Enough, enough, we don't have those
problems, if we did, we'd call the police. Not
you. I thought you guys sold beef."

"We're kind of . . . . a full-service outfit,
Marty."

"Listen, Steak Deluxe! doesn't need security and the meat is up to the Chef. Talk to him."

"We did. He's fine with it. And now, we're talking to you."

"Listen . . . . listen. I'm confused . . . . I need to discuss this with . . . . with the",

Marty could feel his face redden, his hands, shaking, badly.

"Marty, think on this. Get used to it. It's Monday; we'll come back on Wednesday. You'll be on board."

The hand to shake was huge. Marty's hand looked like a child's, inside the catcher's mitt of the stranger.

13

MARTY FOUND CHEF in the Steak Locker. The Chef stood there; eye's closed, swaying ever so slightly.

Marty stopped, didn't say anything. The dry, cold air felt wonderful on his face. It calmed Marty, settled him down. *Jeesus, those guys!*

The Chef came out of his reverie.

"Marty, what are you doing? You look terrible. You need to cut back on the booze."

"Cut back? Are you kidding me? After what I've been through, it's a water glass of Scotch just for starters."

And then Marty went through his meeting with the 'new meat resource.'

Marty went on for a good 10 minutes. Chef listened; he liked the little guy. Liked that Marty came in early, got his job done, went home. He didn't know if his bookkeeper had a wife, kids or even where he lived. Chef's feelings for other people were shallow at best. He did wonder about the black cardigan, grey slacks, white shirt, narrow black tie that Marty wore every day. Like a uniform. Was it the same clothes day after day? Or did he have a pile of shirts and cardigans, all the same, stacked in his closet?

The Chef pushed those thoughts aside. "Let's get you that Scotch." They went up to the deserted bar. He poured Marty 2 fingers of Glenfiddich single malt. Marty downed it in one. Chef poured another; Marty drank half in one gulp.

"Are you better now?"

"Yes, Chef, but you gotta tell me what's going on."

"Marty, I'm sorry. I should have talked to you earlier. With the Councilman taking off, I had to get new financial backing. It's just temporary. Steak Deluxe! is going through a rough patch, but it will all work out." He went on for a bit and sputtered out.

Chef told Marty the bare minimum and even that was mostly false. Marty didn't believe half of it; neither did the Chef.

Marty went home to his house in Alderbrook in east Astoria, to his wife and 2 kids.

When Wednesday came, he took the day off.

When the next Wednesday came, Marty was dead.

14

THE LAST DINERS LEFT STEAK DELUXE! at 9:30pm. Kitchen staff had started breaking down, cleaning up 30 minutes earlier. Restaurants don't stay open late in Astoria. The bar still had a few stragglers.

"Charlie, we had a good night, right?" The Chef and Charlie stood in the kitchen.

"A great night, for a Wednesday, Chef."

"All reservations show?"

"Every single one, it gave us a nice base; walk-ins put us over."

Chef liked to get Charlie's input after every service.

"Any problems I need to know about?"

"Nothing serious Chef, runners could be a bit more attentive."

"Want me to talk to them?"

"No, I'll take care of it." When it came to the staff, the Chef never talked. He screamed, ranted or roared. And always made matters worse.

"I'll see you tomorrow, Charlie."

Chef walked to every station in the kitchen. Correcting, criticizing and complaining. He didn't understand the difference between a leader and a tyrant.

The moment the Chef left the kitchen, the staff was out the door. Everybody had chipped in for a half case of beer; they stood in the parking lot smoking and drinking. Language changed from Kitchen/Spanish to Mexican/Spanish.

Front of house staff headed for Portway Tavern. The Portway is an Astoria landmark. Opened in 1925,

Portway has a charm that's an acquired taste. Small, dark, cozy, with a dedicated group of regulars that see the tavern through slow winter months. Through the front door that never shuts quite right is a long high table on the left side wall where regulars reign. The front of the tavern is all windows which could give a view of Marine Drive if not for the tall Oregon State gambling machines. Against the back wall is the bar and in the center of the room is a collection of mis-matched harvest tables and chairs.

The right side of the Portway has a door, set in the floor with a metal ring inset in the door, flush with the floor. When the Portway sat on piers above the Columbia River, the door was used to *Shanghai* drunken men to outgoing ships in the harbor. Now the Portway sits on solid ground and no one has tried to open the door in years.

Charlie parked in the gravel parking lot behind the Portway. He has Cassi, the receptionist and 2 waiters with him. The rest of the staff came in their own cars.

"I'm always afraid I'll hit those pylons getting out of here," Charlie said.

"They're kind of cool wrapped in those big ship ropes."

"I think of them as a public service; if you don't hit one of them on your way out, you're probably OK to drive."

As they walked into the Portway, an elderly man with a long beard and tam-o'-shanter hat is telling a story at the regular's high table. Charlie stops to listen; he likes Astoria stories.

> "So, I'm sitting outside the Portway, right out on the deck there, facing Marine Drive, enjoying a cold beer on a warm summer afternoon." The gent takes a long pull on the beer in front of him and looks around to make sure his audience is paying attention; they are.

> "All of a sudden there's this horrible noise of shattering glass, I damn near dropped my beer. Then I see the 2nd-floor window on the apartment house across the street got broken out. This guy comes crawling out the window backwards; feet first, face'n the wall. He holds on to the window with both hands, cutting himself on the broken glass. He hangs for a second, there's shouts coming from inside the apartment, he let's go, drops 2 stories to the sidewalk. The sound of the guy landing made me sick, but he gets up and limps away. True story."

> "Alan, that's a hell of a story."

> "Glad you all liked it. I'll see you tomorrow." He says this as he leaves a dollar tip on the table, gets his cane and heads out into the night.

Charlie would have sat with the Steak Deluxe! crew, but there weren't enough chairs. He spots Cassi at the bar, trying to get a drink. The bartender is in the middle of a long discourse with a couple of customers.

> "Guys, I'm telling you I know women. Been married 4 times."

Charlie's been married 3 times and the 3rd is headed down the shitter. The difference between Charlie & the bartender is that Charlie realizes he doesn't know the first thing about women.

> "Hey, Gary, a couple of gin & tonics here, before you launch into the rest of your lecture."

> "Come'n up Charlie."

Drinks in hand, Cassi and Charlie head for the other end of the bar, still standing, no bar stools empty.

> "Thanks for the drink, Charlie. I stood there for 10 minutes, trying to get his attention."

> "Glad I could help."

Shaking his head, Charlie confesses to Cassi that he's the opposite of the bartender.

> "I just don't get women or, for that matter, relationships."

"You just haven't found the right woman yet, Charlie. Look for a woman you can understand".

"Is there a woman like that?"

"Absolutely, Charlie."

"I'm not so sure."

The sheer tonnage of things Charlie doesn't understand is amazing, even when he looks directly at the answer.

15

STEAK DELUXE! IS ONE of the few restaurants to have an aging room. They call it the Steak Locker but call it what you want, its purpose is to age sides of beef before they are cut into entrees.

There was a time when most high-class steak houses would have aging rooms and even a trolley wheeled out to present different cuts to customers. Steak Deluxe! had a trolley in the beginning.

"We have a 20-ounce Bone-in Rib Eye ." The waiter would hold up the steak to each customer at the table. The trolley-man took the Rib Eye back and handed the waiter the next cut.

> "This is our famous T-Bone. 24 ounces of the finest beef."

And so it went, cut after cut of beef, the rest of the entrees and side dishes. Even the vegetables.

> "Our carrots are organically grown in Knappa."

Enough with the show and tell, Charlie thought.

> "Chef, we need to lose the Trolley show. Let's sell some food, turn some tables."

The Chef had to agree, reluctantly.

> "But there's no way I'm getting rid of the Steak Locker, if it goes, I'm gone."

Most restaurants moved away from aging rooms and trolleys, not only to save money but because of a culture change. Diners appreciate good food and are willing to pay for it, but they don't want to know about the way it got to their plate. Don't want to know about the suffering that went into it. The distance between animal and dish needs to be sizable.

16

CHERRY JOHNSON CAME from the Hoquiam Police Department in coastal Washington State. She was part of an unusual trade between Hoquiam and Astoria PD's. Astoria sent 2 patrolmen north, Hoquiam sent a patrol officer and Detective Johnson south to Astoria.

"Hi, I'm the player to be named later."

"Huh?"

Cherry was introducing herself to the Desk Sargent at Astoria PD.

Her next stop, the Chief's office, a meeting there, then an introduction to the on-duty staff, followed by lunch with the Chief and Mayor. Cherry would be the highest-ranking female officer on the force; in fact, the only female on the force.

Although she held the rank of Detective, Cherry's first week of service was a ride-along with Senior Patrolman, Hal Evans. It was a good idea. Cherry got a lay of the land in Astoria and a run-down on the Police Department and most of the citizens living in Astoria.

Hal is a solid cop; he likes patrol, does it well. It's all he wanted. Not interested in moving up in the Department, too much politics, too little policing. Hal had 2 years to go on his 20 years of police service; then he was done. Retirement sounded better and better each month.

Cherry had caused quite a stir in the Astoria Police Department. Young, good looking, plus the only female on the force. That's all it took for rumors, off-color jokes and worse. Hal acted as her protector until he realized she didn't need it.

The call came in at 12:30am, a fight in the parking lot of Dirty Dan's involving 3 males. Hal took the call,

"Car 2 responding, lights, no siren". The fight in full swing when the patrol car pulled up; 2 guys punching a 3rd. But the 3rd, giving as good as he got.

"Hal, I'll take care of this, finish your coffee." Cherry didn't have an Astoria PD uniform yet; she wore her Hoquiam patrol uniform, the Hoquiam ID replaced with Astoria's ID, and an Astoria PD badge. She had lightened her on-body gear to radio, firearm, baton, cuffs. All she needed.

"Ok boys, let's break it up."

"Who's the hell are you?"

"She's a goddamn bitch cop."

Both replies are slurred, all 3 men drunk; mean drunk.

"OK, boys, 2nd time, let's stop and you can head home."

Outnumbered, the 3rd drunk fighter takes this pause to re-group, vomit, hands on his knees, breathing hard between retches.

The other 2 spread out and move towards Cherry in a menacing, if not entirely stable, manner.

"What did you say, BITCH?"

"OK boys, if it's gonna go that way, let's do this first." Cherry removed the baton from her belt and offered it to the nearest drunk.

"Here, take this."

"Why?"

"Because I want the dead guy's fingerprints on my baton. Showing I was in mortal danger when I shot him."

The advance slowed, then came to a swaying stop. Cherry's meaning percolated into their brains. Heads down, they walked away but could be heard mumbling 'about bitch cops' and how lucky for her they'd 'been drunk or we'd kicked her ass.'

"She's got a nice ass."

"Shut up, stupid."

As those 2 stumbled off, against all odds, the 3rd straightened up and made a headfirst lunge at Cherry.

"You are kind'a cute honey . . ."

He had an arm out trying to get a hand on Cherry's breast or her PD badge, hard to say which.

The moment he came close, Cherry moved ever so slightly left, grabbed the extended arm with both hands and let his forward momentum carry him past her as she shoved the arm behind his back, then sharply up. Just short of the breaking point.

"GOD DAMN, you're hurting me . . ."

His arm went up a couple of degrees.

"Shut up and I'll explain things."

"LET GO. . . LET GO. . . DAMN YOU." Just short of screaming.

In a graceful movement, Cherry brought her foot down on the backside of his knee. Firmly, but not as hard as she could have.

The kneecap hit the graveled parking lot hard.

"Now can I talk?" She leaned down, speaking softly.

"Yes . . . yes."

The voice wavered, struggled.

"Good, there are two ways this can go. You can get up; I'll help you, we'll walk to the police car . . . or . . . you can be carried to the cruiser, bloody with a broken arm, your choice."

"I'll walk, I'll walk."

Hal Evans watched all this from the patrol car. From that night on, Cherry Johnson was a solid, respected member of the Astoria Police Department.

17

CHARLIE HAD GIVEN UP on days-off a long time ago. Sure, some days he came in a little later, other days he left work early. But basically, every day that ended in a 'Y' is a workday for Charlie. This day he got out of bed around 8am, in time for the 2nd hour of the Today Show. He wondered, is Savannah Guthrie cuter than Jane Pauley in her prime? Who was the weather guy before Al Roker? Why did he remember the name, Gene Shallot? He pondered this while munching on day-old (or older?) pizza from Geno's.

His thoughts moved on to his wife, soon to be ex-wife. The fact that his life didn't change much when she left didn't shock Charlie. Didn't even surprise him; just reminded him of the separate lives they both led. Charlie was a loner, always had been, even as a child. And now alone, again.

It seemed natural to him, almost comforting.

Charlie got to Steak Deluxe! around 9am. He said hi to the kitchen crew on the way to his office. On his desk, a note from Marty, another shortage in the Steak Locker.

Why doesn't Marty move his goddamn desk into the Steak Locker and leave me the hell alone?

But Charlie, being Charlie, knows Marty is right. It's either someone stealing, again, or bad bookkeeping. Only an idiot would bet on the latter instead of the former.

Charlie wearily walked into Marty's office; the only office smaller than his.

Marty sat upright in his chair, his head slightly down, with a hole in the middle of his head.

Neatly, centered between his eyes.

Good God Almighty, what in the hell is going on? 2 murders . . . . . 2 murders? That's probably more than Astoria's had in a decade.

Charlie didn't shout or scream; the noise, all in his head.

Both murders here at Steak Deluxe! And because of me, the police will only know about this one, unless I tell them about the first.

And why in the world didn't I say anything about the first murder, the Councilman? The police are going to think I did it, murdered him. No . . . . no, they'll think I did them both. But I didn't do anything. It just looks like I did.

The perfect suspect, me!

Suspect? Me? That's not all of it. I'm the next guy to be killed . . . the next guy. It's like the killer or killers are moving up the food chain at Steak Deluxe! The next one killed is me or the Chef.

All too much for Charlie. He was exhausted from arguing with himself.

He'd do the right thing, call Chef, then the police. Charlie thought of a drink first but reconsidered. Booze on the breath of a guy calling in a murder at 9am might seem odd to the law.

Or worse, exactly what a guilty guy would do.

18

CALL OF A SHOOTING VICTIM at Steak Deluxe! came in at 9:13am. 2 patrol units responded, lights and sirens, guns drawn. The scene secured; patrol called the Chief. His initial walk-through over, Chief Evans called Detective Johnson at home, it is her day off.

> "Cherry, we need you at Steak Deluxe! now. There's been a shooting."

She arrived at the crime scene 10 minutes later wearing jeans and a sweatshirt, hair in a ponytail, badge attached to her belt.

Chief Evans took Detective Johnson to look at the murder site. A police photographer still shooting the scene. After a few minutes, the Chief and Cherry had the start of a headache from the camera flash.

"Seen enough, Detective?"

"Yeah, but now I can't see anything. Damn flash. Give me a second to get my retinas working again."

It didn't take any great sleuthing to determine what happened. Somebody shot poor Marty right between the eyes from a distance of 5 to 6 feet. Not self-inflicted; it would be a hell of a reach for a guy to shoot himself in the head from 6 feet away. This was murder, pure and simple.

Now the questions were; who did it and why?

"OK Cherry, it's always 1 of 3 things in a murder; love, money or hate. What do you think? Give me your first impressions."

Chief Evans and Lieutenant Johnson were standing in the restaurant's kitchen now.

"Here's what we know, Chief. I talked with the manager for a minute before the walk-through, sounds like the dead guy was happily married to a cute wife, 2 adorable kids and a bungalow in Alderbrook. But that doesn't mean he didn't have somebody on the side. We'll investigate love and hate angles in the interviews.

"It looks like the victim; he's the bookkeeper here, was setting up cash drawers when he got shot. Cash is still on top of the desk. So, the money angle's out, not sure about love and hate yet."

"Thanks Detective, any questions for me?"

"Time of death, Chief?"

"Not official but looks like less than 2 hours."

"So, somebody waltzes in here around 7am, shoots a guy in the head and walks out the door. Hell, of a start to the workday. Anybody else here around 7?"

"Crew here in the kitchen around 8, the restaurant manager called it in when he got to work around 9."

"Well, Chief, despite what the manager said, my first guess is a jealousy shooting. Workplace-romance, maybe somebody screwing somebody else's wife. Like I said, we can try and sort that out in the interviews."

It sounds like she is done, but she isn't.

"Maybe a jealousy thing but . . . I got kind of a hunch . . . it almost feels like it's a warning."

"Cherry, I'm thinking the same thing."

Basic police protocol was followed from the get-go. First responding patrol officers secured the crime scene and cleared the building. Coroner called, determination of death made; gunshot to the head (not a big surprise). The weapon, most likely a 38-caliber revolver, fired from close range.

The restaurant staff let back in the restaurant; interviews started. They went as interviews usually did, contradictory, confusing and in general, not all that helpful.

"Marty . . . . Marty? Really? Why?"

"Nicest guy in the world."

"Kind of a prick at times."

"Marty kept to himself. Worked hard, didn't say much".

"He said I punched in before my shift; it was a mistake. I told him that, but he made a big deal out of it, got Charlie involved. It pissed me off. But I didn't kill him. You don't think I did it? Do you?"

"Oh My God! Marty? Killed? Was he married?"

"Did he have kids?"

The last 2 people interviewed were Charlie and the Chef.

Charlie sweated through his interview. Not just perspiration, full-on flop sweat. He looked like Nixon during a Watergate press conference. Detective Johnson asked a patrolman to bring Charlie a bar towel. The patrolman brought 3.

"Charlie, do you want to take a break? Maybe do this later today at the station?" Cherry became a little worried. The sweat, one thing, but the jugular vein bulging out of his neck, a whole other deal. She didn't need murder and a heart attack all in one day.

"No, no, I want to get this over. I've never seen a dead body before. I liked Marty . . . . a lot."

Charlie wasn't entirely truthful, yes, he did like Marty but he'd seen a murder victim before. Just a few days ago. His heart beat so loud he worried the Detective would hear it.

Why didn't I tell them about the 1st murder? Can't do it now, they'll think I did both. What the hell am I doing?

Instantly, the next sickening thought;

I'm next. Knife in my chest? Bullet between my eyes? I'm the next dead guy.

With these gruesome thoughts charging through his head, Charlie had a hard time answering the most basic questions. If he wasn't a suspect, to begin with, Charlie felt he is now.

Sweating for a different reason, Chef had a damn good hunch what happened to Marty, but he kept it to himself. The Chef had been in tight situations before; he fared better than Charlie in his interview.

19

THE FIRST MAJOR CRIMES MEETING was held at police headquarters after restaurant interviews finished. Attending was the Chief, the Assistant District Attorney, Senior Patrolman Hal Evans and Lt. Detective Cherry Johnson.

When first announced in the Astorian newspaper, comment around town on the Major Crimes Unit;

> "Major Crimes, what's that in Astoria, over-time parking?'

"You'd be surprised," was Chief Jacob's reply.

The Chief walked into the meeting, knowing exactly why this unit is needed.

Once everyone coffee'd up, with yellow legal pads and Bic pens ready, the meeting begins.

"I'm putting Detective Johnson in charge of this investigation. The investigation will take over this interrogation room, it will be secure. Always locked; you will get keys. I want this wrapped up quickly, all details closely held. Any leaks will be deemed insubordination and cause for dismissal. I will make a statement to the press late this afternoon; there will be no further statements until I decide it appropriate."

It was the longest speech Chief Jacobs had ever made.

"Lt. Detective Johnson, do you understand my orders?"

"Yes sir."

The Chief asked the Senior Patrolman the same question and got the same answer. Assistant District Attorney, Sam Abrams, didn't report to the Chief, so it wasn't a question asked. More like a pronouncement:

"Joe, any leaks from the DA's office and there will be one hell of a price to pay, from both you and the DA."

Joe had a quick response. "Tell me one time there has been a leak from our department . . . . ."

"Do you want a list?"

"Chief, Joe, do we have time for this?" Cherry could be a leader too.

"When do you want updates, Chief?"

"Thank you, Detective, 3 times a day. Morning, noon and night or whenever events warrant."

"Yes sir."

The Chief left the room. Cherry looked at Joe, the assistant DA and Hal, the patrol officer;

"OK boys, let's do some police work."

20

CHERRY JOHNSON HAD an unusual upbringing. She was the first and thankfully only child of a 'hippie' couple. Her parents were terrible at parenting. Cherry's mom gave birth in a tent at a commune east of Tacoma. A commune member 'Earth Mother' mid-wife attended the birth.

Cherry's parents married after her birth; the wedding officiated by the commune's founder. All this happened at the end of the 'Age of Aquarius.'

Cherry was lucky to survive her birth and early years. Commune lifestyle and hygiene were iffy at best, downright dangerous at worst, especially for a newborn. By the time Cherry was a toddler, she became a precocious, independent being. When she started to talk, she called her parents, Ed and Jill, at their request, not Mom and Dad. It came out as one word, *Ed'nJill.* In addition to her parents, an ever-changing group of commune characters watched over her. But no one had responsibility for Cherry; for her health, welfare, or anything else.

At age 8, Cherry had never been to school, never seen a doctor or dentist. She couldn't read or write but could sing almost every Grateful Dead song. And she learned to play the ukulele. Singing *Over the Rainbow*, accompanying herself on the ukulele, was her go-to for attention.

Then things changed for the better. Cherry's grandparents finally tracked down their only grandchild. They gave Ed and Jill a thousand dollars to basically go away and leave Cherry. The money was the price they paid for their grandchild.

For the next 3 years, Cherry had a typical mid-American upbringing. A private tutor got her up to grade level. Basic health care and regular meals got her health back. She loved going to school, the books, teachers, kids her age.

In short, she flourished.

At age 11, all of that changed when the grandparents died. The grandfather died first of a heart attack. The grandmother died 8 months later of a broken heart.

Cherry's parents were back in the picture. Ed'nJill hoped for a grand inheritance, the answer for everything. There was some inheritance, but most of it went to Cherry and not until she turned 21.

Ed and Jill took this out on their daughter; they viewed it as Cherry's fault. With their meager inheritance, Ed and Jill bought an ancient school bus. For the next 4 years, this became home for the 3 of them.

Ed and Jill had been through the *'Summer of Love'* and the *'Age of Aquarius.'* They embraced both. Now they were in the *'Age of Drugs.'* First cocaine, then crack cocaine, next methedrine, which they both smoked and produced in the school bus. All of this in front of their child. Cherry became the responsible person in the family. She became the parent, to her parents.

And it all came to a crashing halt, in a back street of downtown Bellingham, Washington. A meter-maid, posting another parking ticket on the school bus front window, heard screaming coming from inside the bus. After kicking in the locked glass doors, she found a man dead and a teenager trying to revive a woman, apparently unconscious from an overdose.

Next for Cherry was a 3-year trip through Washington State foster care. After a couple of false starts, she became a member of a warm, giving family. A couple with 3 kids of their own and 2 adopted, made room in their home and life for Cherry. The family had many additions, 1 more not a big issue.

Cherry stayed with this family for a year. The year grounded her, resurrected her spirit, got her will back. She stayed in touch with the family and felt a part of it for the rest of her life.

When Cherry turned 18, she had choices to make. Her foster family had a rule about that birthday. At 18, it was time to find your way. And Cherry was ready. She could stay in Bellingham, get a job or go to college. Living through all the changes in her short life, Cherry wanted one thing, a structured and secure environment.

She found it in the Army.

21

"So, Cherry, Army?"

"Yup."

"Thought so."

"How about you?"

"Yup."

"Thought so."

This discussion between Hal Evans and Cherry started, after going for coffee at McDonald's drive-thru. Neither were ones for long, drawn-out conversations.

"Afghanistan, Cherry?"

"Yeah, 2 tours. How about you?"

"8 years in the Army when I was young and stupid."

"And now Hal, you're older and . . . . ?"

"Older and still not the sharpest knife in the drawer. What'd you do after Afghanistan?"

"A tour in Iraq as an MP. Then back in the States as an MP out of Joint Base Lewis/McChord. Stayed there until my hitch was up."

"Didn't re-up," Hal didn't say this as a question, more of a statement.

"Thought about it but didn't. Didn't mind the Army, guess I needed a change. By the way, this is the worst coffee."

"No, it's the best coffee in town; everybody knows that."

This was a continuing debate. They traded coffee spots, Cherry's favorites were 3 Cups and Coffee Girl. With Hal, it's always McDonald's.

"How'd you end up in Hoquiam?"

"For a nice guy, Hal, you sure are one questioning son-of-a-bitch."

"Just trying to be sociable."

"Hoquiam was the first to offer a job. I wanted a small-town force. I'd seen enough gnarly shit in Afghanistan and Iraq. I wanted to coast for a while. Can we get some real coffee Hal?"

"No. What's Hoquiam PD like?"

"Their force was going through kind of a mini-scandal, let go of 3 or 4 people. Because of that, I worked my way up fast, made Detective in 3 years. A record."

"Good for you. Why'd you leave?"

"Got tired of coasting. Wanted to see the bright lights of Astoria, a little bit better pay and, of course, you Hal!"

"I'm not enough to make a woman walk across the street."

"That's not what your wife says."

"I sure don't know what she sees in me. I'm a little afraid one day she's gonna take a long look at me, walk out the door and keep on going."

"Not likely, Hal. You're a good man. They're hard to find."

22

"Hello, Mrs. Brock."

"Please call me Missy, Chief Jacobs."

The Chief of Police, Sam Jacobs, had met the Councilman's wife at Steak Deluxe! and various social functions around town.

"Missy it is. And who is this with you?"

The tall, 60-something gentleman with grey hair and beard answered for her.

"I'm James Stone; I represent Mrs. Brock in a matter we'd like to discuss with you."

The elegant man reminded Chief Jacobs of a former US Secretary of State; he couldn't remember which one.

"Very good. Please step into my office and we can talk."

The lawyer spoke first,

"We have an issue that could negatively affect Mr. and Mrs. Brock's standing in the community. We are asking for discretion on the part of yourself and your department."

That statement exceeded the Chief's level for formalities.

"First, I need to know, what we're talking about__"

"My husband ran off. . . " This came out high pitched and wavering, Missy on the verge of tears.

"Ran off?"

"Yes, ran off. I haven't seen or talked to my husband in 3 weeks." Missy was crying now.

"And you waited until now to come to the police?" The Chief asked this as he looked slowly from Missy to her lawyer.

The lawyer answered,

> "Mrs. Brock had every reason to believe the Councilman would return home . . . . in a reasonable period of time."

> "A reasonable period would be 2 or 3 days, wouldn't it, Missy? Now, we're 3 weeks in and it makes it much harder for my department."

> "It's . . . . it's just so, so, embarrassing. He's done this before, I just thought he'd come to his senses. If this gets out, I'm the talk of the town. It's, it's humiliating!"

> *This woman has a high threshold for humiliation,* 'the Chief thought. *'He's been a wild womanizer around this town forever.'*

Chief Jacobs kept these thoughts to himself.

> "I'll bring my detective in on this," the Chief reached for his intercom. "Mike, have Lt. Johnson come in, please."

> "Chief Jacobs, we need to keep this between the 3 of us. Discretion is everything." The lawyer again.

"Well, Jim__"

"Actually, it's James, Chief Jacobs."

"Actually, it's like this, Jim. You stick to lawyering and I'll stick to police work."

Cherry came in, introductions made. She sensed a level of tension in the room.

23

AFTER 3 DAYS OF DIGGING, Detective Cherry Johnson had nothing on the Councilman's disappearance. And today was the briefing with the Chief.

"OK, Detective, what have you got?"

"Not much Chief. To be honest . . . . nothing."

"I expect you to be honest, Detective. But I was expecting something."

"You and me both, Chief. This guy didn't run or hide; he vanished."

"Well if he vanished, the question is, did the bastard do it on his own or was it due to foul play? Hell, half the husbands in this town would like to cause him lethal damage."

"I'll get to that in a bit. First, let me give you the run-down we did. With the wife's permission, we looked at all their credit and debit cards; there were a lot of both. No use by the Councilman after his disappearance and nothing unusual beforehand. Checked all bank records, at 2 banks in Astoria and 2 more in Portland. Nothing unusual. I checked the couple's safety deposit boxes. All in order, nothing missing."

"Well, Cherry, you did your due diligence there. What about phone records?"

"Checked the landline, both of his cell phones and the wife's; nothing since the afternoon of his disappearance."

"Could have a burner phone."

"Yes, there is that Chief. Could be using a burner, impossible to know."

"Foul play . . . ?"

"Without a body, can't tell, Chief. And you're right, according to the gossip around town, there are plenty of men and women, that would like to see harm done to the Councilman. Beat up, broken limbs, maybe castration with a rusty knife."

"Ouch . . . ." The Chief repositioned himself in his chair.

"But as far as actual leads, Chief, nothing. Just conjecture and gossip. The strongest is an incident at Steak Deluxe! last year. The Councilman was hitting on one of the waitresses. There was talk of a hot affair. Her husband, one of the bartenders at the restaurant. The husband took exception to the Councilman's advances and called him out. At the bar, during Happy Hour. In front of a full bar, the aggrieved husband grabbed the Councilman by the necktie and drug him over the bar top. Tried to get the Councilman's hand in the blender, but the plug was pulled before he could turn it on."

"Would have loved to seen that."

"Me too, Chief. No charges filed. The bartender got fired; dragging a customer over the bar, even if said customer deserves it, is a firing offense. Bartender and waitress got divorced, she carried on with the Councilman for a while and then he moved on to someone new."

"Did you check into the bartender?"

"Yep, he's living in Vegas, bartending at the Rio. No wants, no warrants. Just got remarried."

"That was fast."

"He's a good-looking guy, Chief. I remember seeing him around town. Plus, love happens fast in Vegas; it's why they have 24-hour wedding chapels."

"Keep me posted, Detective."

"Will do, Chief."

24

CHARLIE CHECKED THE INVENTORY REPORT against the produce on the shelf in the walk-in cooler. Another shortage, this time mushrooms. At least not steaks for once.

But the damn mushroom's cost almost as much as the steaks.

Charlie's counting and cursing was disturbed by a sound he couldn't place. He shook it off. There it was again, louder now. Charlie walked to the back of the cooler, the always locked Steak Locker door stood slightly open. The sound came from the Locker. Charlie stuck his head through the door, no sound. He waited; there it was again. He went into the Locker.

What he saw, he couldn't comprehend. *Some sort of LSD flashback?* Charlie closed his eyes, opened them again. Saw the same thing. 2 enormous hams, shockingly white, moving up and down, in sync. *We haven't had ham on the menu in months. We're a damn Steak House.*

Charlie wanted to look away but couldn't. The scene was mesmerizing. Finally, it clicked.

The Councilman's wife on a sack of oysters, the Chef on top of her. Now that he knew what he was seeing, it was worse for Charlie.

The Councilman's wife saw Charlie over the Chef's shoulder and screamed. Chef took this as encouragement, redoubling his efforts. Charlie would have screamed too, but his voice didn't work. He stumbled out of the Locker.

I am never, ever going in the damn Steak Locker by myself. EVER.

That night at the pre-service meeting, Charlie told the wait-staff;

"Don't push the oysters."

25

CHARLIE, CHEF AND THE CHEF'S LATEST CONQUEST
sat drinking at the bar after dinner service. The Chef
and the much younger woman left together after a
couple of drinks. Charlie started turning off lights, he
found Cassi at the Reception desk, mumbling darkly
at her computer.

> "Hey Cassi, I thought you went home an hour
> ago."

> "Something happened to the reservation
> software program. Just got it running again."

"Good for you, Cassi."

There was a silence between the 2. This was the first time they had been alone. Still at work, but alone.

Charlie spoke first.

"Do you remember the guy that came in late with a date and another guy?"

"Yeah, really late. 2 jerks and a woman that needs to adjust her taste in men."

"Well, they sent back a bottle of the Sandberg Vineyard Pinot, said it was too warm."

"The Pinot from Big Table winery?"

"Yep, it's sitting open behind the bar. Would you like a sip?"

"No, thank you."

Charlie felt his face growing red.

"But, a nice full glass would be delightful." She said it with a chuckle.

Charlie felt embarrassed by how relieved he felt.

They sat at the bar, the lighted shelves under the liquor bottles providing a warm, soft glow.

"We had a good turn-over tonight."

"Charlie, we're not talking business, are we?"

And they didn't talk business. They talked about everything else. Cassi about growing up in Kansas and how she ended up in Astoria; bad luck with men, 1 in college and another after graduation. That took the first 2 glasses of wine.

Charlie's mid-West upbringing finished the rest of the bottle. The hour they spent together went by quickly.

"Boy, that was good. Thanks, Charlie."

"Glad you liked it. I have a split of better."

"Better than that is hard to believe."

Charlie got 2 fresh glasses, specifically shaped to bring out highlights of the wine.

"Try a sip first; leave it in your mouth for a second."

"Man-o-man, Charlie, this is better."

They talked softly back and forth for another hour. The split-bottle gone; Charlie went behind the bar to dig out another special bottle.

"Thanks, Charlie, but we need to go home now. It's late."

Cassi called a cab, Charlie finished turning out the lights.

She lived in a 'compact,' actually tiny, 100-year-old house halfway up one of the many hills in Astoria. After a short ride to her home, the cab pulled up to the curb.

Charlie leaned in close. Cassi expected a kiss and got a question instead.

"Are you going to invite me in?"

There was a long minute of silence. The cab driver took the opportunity to light a cigarette. He seemed to be enjoying the moment.

"Well, I could invite you in Charlie, we'd have a great time and be in love, or at least lust for a week or two. We'd be the talk of the restaurant. Then it would be over. Just awkward moments at work, and one of us would have to find another job and that person would be me, wouldn't it?"

Charlie's only move; stay silent. She was exactly right.

"If you're interested in something serious, wait a week and we can go on a grown-up date. If you ask me out with a post-it note at the reception desk, I'll never talk to you again."

"Can I walk you to your door." *At least I'm a gentleman,* Charlie thought.

"I can make it, I'm not so sure about you, but thanks."

She gave Charlie a chaste kiss on the cheek and walked to her door.

The cab driver flipped the cigarette butt out the window.

"She told you, man."

26

THE NEXT DAY Charlie waited at the bar for a post-dinner service briefing with the Chef. He was still in the kitchen, berating the staff for various misdeeds.

"Bernie, give me a Jack Daniels on the rocks, would ya?"

"Sure Charlie, but I have to tell you, drinking can cause memory loss, or worse, memory loss."

"Huh?"

"Nothing Charlie, drink up."

The Chef showed up 2 drinks later. The agenda, always the same; reservations and did they show? Number of covers (number of plates served), gross volume for the dining room, gross for the bar. Both figures compared to last year.

"How'd the Asian tenderloin go over?"

"So-so, Chef."

"What's the problem?"

"Too Asian."

From there, the conversation went to the top 2 topics; women or sports. Oddly enough, the topic is never women in sports. Tonight's theme, women.

The Chef talking;

"I discovered that to women a man cooking is very seductive. I'd invite them over to my place for dinner, never on the first date, but after that."

"She'd show up; I'd be at the stove. We'd have a glass of wine as I finished cooking and set the table. More wine with dinner, maybe a cordial with dessert, then it's off to the races."

"Only a couple of times it didn't work. Worst was after wine, the dinner and dessert the chick says, 'I've got another date, I'm late now.'

"But mostly, it worked like magic. But even then, if the relationship lasted more than a couple of months, the woman would start to resent my cooking."

'Too spicy, no taste needs salt, too salty, needs spice, too rare, not rare enough.'

"I'm a Chef 20 years, working in the best restaurants in the country and she's telling me how to cook; a woman that couldn't boil water. She's telling me."

27

CHEF AND THE 2 FINNISH GIANTS met in the Chef's office. One of the giants sat in the Chef's chair behind the desk. The other one (*were they twins?*) stood by the desk. Chef stood halfway out the door of his own office, in his own restaurant.

> "We came over to make sure we're on the same page here. It looks like things got squared away with Marty, the bookkeeper."

"HE WAS SHOT IN THE HEAD!" The Chef shouted that, then, in a whisper, repeated it. "Shot . . . . in the head!"

"Like I said, Chef, squared away. Too bad, seemed like a good guy. Now we need to get square with you."

Christ Almighty . . . what did that mean? The Chef leaned against the doorframe for support.

One of the giants spoke,

"We bought out your original investors a while ago; now we're taking over the money part of the business. One of us will be here at closing every night to take the deposit."

"I take the deposit." The Chef's voice seemed far away.

"You used to take the deposit. Now we do. This will work better if you just listen to what I'm telling you."

"But I . . ."

"Look at me, Chef."

Chef stared at his new business partners, then lowered his eyes. Nothing said.

"Chef, the schedule is changing; you're open 7 days a week now."

The Chef had a hard time getting his head around that. Restaurant hours were Tuesday through Saturday; Lunch to Close, Brunch only on Sunday.

"The staffing cost is going to kill us."

"Figure it out, Chef. Make it work. Also, we're both pulling a salary, starting today."

"There is no way the business can take on 2 mor__"

"Well, you're saving Marty's salary. You'll make it work Chef . . . you need to keep square with us."

28

ANOTHER CONVERSATION between Senior Patrolman Hal Evans and Detective Cherry Johnson, this time at Coffee Girl.

"So, Cherry, that's some kind of nickname."

"Cherry isn't a nickname; it's my given name."

"Did you piss off your parents at birth?"

"My parents were stoned, drunk or both my entire life. I guess they thought my name was cute or at least funny."

'Yikes, sorry I brought it up. Have you forgiven them yet?"

"Forgive them? Maybe. My Dad died of a heroin overdose. I haven't talked with my Mom in years."

"I'm sorry . . . ."

"Don't be, but I've got to go, if you have any other questions about my name, ask now.'

"Well . . . what was it like growing up with the name Cherry? Must have been some mean jokes."

"Not so bad in school, but later some people would give me a hard time. But only once."

"Only once?"

"Yeah, I tried laughing remarks away, or ignoring people, but it's just easier to settle it."

"Settle it?"

"I broke a guy's jaw in a bar once. Didn't hurt his 2 friends as bad, but they didn't get up either. I'm a hard hitter."

"OK, I've heard enough."

Hal and Cherry tried to have coffee a couple of times a week. Cherry relied on Hal for Astoria knowledge and Police Department info. Hal treated her like the daughter he didn't have. Admittedly a hard-ass sister, but still a sister who needed his help.

He couldn't figure out why Cherry didn't like McDonald's and its coffee. Sure, he liked Coffee Girl, appreciated the great view of the Columbia from the end of Pier 39. But dammit, the coffee is just too strong. After a couple of cups, he felt like he could skip the patrol car and run the rest of his shift.

During these chats, Hal sensed that deep down, Cherry needed to bring justice to wrong-doers. Yes, she liked the action and yes, she is an adrenaline junkie. And sometimes action, adrenaline and justice did come together.

The cop job met her immediate needs; rent, food, car payments for a used, lovingly cared for Corvette Sting Ray. But the driving force for Cherry is the pursuit of justice.

29

CHERRY FELT TIRED after a long day. One of the disadvantages of being Detective; no over-time. She stopped at Merry Time Bar & Grill anyway. The name confused Cherry; she would have liked the spelling Maritime better. *'But I don't own the bar, do I?'*

The Merry Time is getting to be her 'regular.' She likes the big space, the people and the food. At the bar, Cherry rediscovered her talent and love of pool. She didn't play often, doesn't want the reputation as a pool shark. But that's what she is. When she does play, she doesn't lose. If her opponent is male, and it usually is, it brings out a 'killer instinct.' If there is money on the table, it's lights out for the opponent.

Cherry walked up to the bar, smiled at the bartender;

"Hey, Joni."

"Hey, Cherry! What are you having?"

"Well, what do you think I need, Joni?"

"From here behind the bar, it looks like you need 10 hours of sleep, with a bit of manly attention beforehand. But we discourage sleeping here and the manly quotient is a little low tonight. So, I'm bringing you a cold, tall Pilsner from Buoy Beer."

Joni was right; the Pilsner is just what Cherry needed.

"Good choice, thanks, Joni."

"You're welcome. Forgot to tell you, there's a co-worker of yours in the corner. Been here a while, I'm getting a little worried."

Cherry spotted Hal Evans hunched over in a booth in the corner. He was alone. One of the many interesting things with men is that when they drink, the first tell is their hair. If Hal was as drunk as his hair, this could be a problem. Cherry had never seen

Hal in a bar before. Didn't know he drank, just assumed he didn't.

They'd stopped serving him alcohol, coffee only, from here on. Cherry got this from Joni, the nearer she got to the booth, Cherry understood why.

"Hey Hal, what are you doing here?"

"I'm sit'n here, sitting here, drinking, trying to forget."

"That'd be a hell of a country song, Hal, but really what are you doing here?"

"I told you. What are you do'n, doing?"

"Well, as it turns out, I'm here to drive you home."

"I'm gonna walk, Cherry."

"OK, but before you go, do you always get a country drawl when you drink?"

"I'm, I'm talking normal-ish."

"No, you're not. And I'm guessing you aren't thinking normal either. Drink some more of that coffee; I don't want to drop you off at home like this."

Hal's phone had been buzzing. Now Cherry's started.

"Hello."

"Cherry, it's Grace, Hal's wife, is he with you?"

Grace knew the question came off wrong, too harsh, off base. But she knows it's the day. The day from long ago, that won't go away, can't be forgotten. Some years it goes by with nothing more than anguish. Some years it's bad, this could be one of those years. Grace knew she needed to get on top of it, now, before it gets worse.

Today was an anniversary, the day years ago their son, Sammy died.

"Grace, I'll bring him home, let him get straightened out a bit first."

"I need him home, now."

30

SAMMY WAS HAL and Grace's 2nd child. He was the good child. Slept through the night as a new-born, walked early, talked early. Helpful, kind, outgoing, the perfect little boy. Even during his teen years, when all his friends turned into people their parents could barely recognize, Sammy didn't change. And that continued for all his short life,

Hal and Graces first-born, Hal Jr., was the exact opposite of Sammy. Colicky, awake every couple of hours through the night, the early years were not easy for son or parents. And it never got any easier. Countless parent/teacher meetings, suspensions, expulsions; school years were a nightmare. After graduation, it got worse. College, not an option, Junior tried and failed at retail, landscaping, commercial fishing and a dozen more hiring's. And firings.

He did excel at HBO series-binging and couch surfing. Junior laid claim to the basement and sometimes didn't surface for days; then only when the refrigerator down there ran out of food. Grace went down once a month. Hal Sr. didn't ever go down there.

During all of this, Sammy remained on course, never wavered. The striking difference made it worse for Hal Jr. If he needed a living, breathing example of how screwed-up he was, Junior only had to look at his brother.

Hal Jr. barely graduated from Grant High School in Portland. It seemed like the main reason he did graduate was the school was done with him. Junior's GPA, 1.7

Four years younger, Sammy breezed through high school, took college requirement courses in his junior and senior years. What Grant High School had to offer, Sammy took advantage of. Sammy was on the honor roll all 4 years of high school. He took both

French and Spanish classes and was President of the French Club. Also, Class President as a senior.

Sammy was a good basketball player, but not great; he dropped out of the program in his junior year, so a more talented sophomore could get a chance. Sammy did continue to practice with the team at the coach's request. And he played varsity baseball his last two years of high school. Didn't start much, but that was all right. Sammy liked the camaraderie, liked practices better than the games. He loved the smell of newly mown grass and the sound of the bat on a ball, watching as it sailed out to him in right field during warm-up.

Sammy graduated with a GPA of 4.3, the unusually high grading due to the advanced classes and college requirement courses he took. Teachers who had taught both Evan's brothers couldn't believe they were related.

An academic scholarship from a private college in Portland was awarded to Sammy. He had an internship at the local newspaper for the summer. Sammy was looking forward to graduation and the associated festivities.

The graduation party that Grant high school put on was designed to be an alternative to the wild, drunken and dangerous private parties sure to be thrown. The gym got decorated, parents dragooned into being chaperones, food catered and a band hired. Once kids entered the gym, they couldn't leave and return. Once you went in, you were there for the night. Cots would be set up. Breakfast served the next morning in the cafeteria.

There was kind of a challenge to see who could stay up the latest. Sammy was one of the last ones standing. He finally gave in at 4am.

Breakfast did little to wake Sammy up. He had driven 4 of his friends to the party and now, at 7:30am, he was taking them home. He wanted to sleep longer, but one of his buddies was leaving early for vacation.

"OK. Everybody wake-up, get in the car!"

"Gees, Sammy you get grumpy without sleep."

"Grumpy or not, I'm your ride home and it beats walking."

The accident call came into Portland PD dispatch at 7:38am.

"2 vehicle accident, North-East 33rd and Broadway. Injuries reported, entrapment possible. Sending crash unit and ambulance. Patrol respond."

"Patrol 16 responding, I'll take it." Hal Evan's patrol car was only 3 minutes away.

The accident reconstruction report showed Sammy's car ran through a red light, collided with a car in the intersection and then hit a light pole head-on. Sammy and his front-seat passenger died on impact. The 2 in the back seat had severe but not life-threatening injuries. The driver who had the green light, suffered minor injuries. All concerned were wearing seatbelts.

The most likely cause of the accident; the driver, Sammy Evans, fell asleep at the wheel.

31

SAMMY'S DEATH TORE the Evans family apart. The months after his death and funeral rushed by in a murderous fog. When they came out the other side, Grace and Hal's marriage was over. Hal Jr. dropped out of sight. His parents didn't hear from him for 2 years.

Hal quit his job with the Portland Police Department. It was a close call whether he'd quit or get fired. Once Grace left him, his drinking soared out of control. His career at Portland PD down the drain.

Hal and Grace never got divorced; they were too tired for that. They lived separately, didn't see each other and didn't talk. What was left to say?

Gradually it changed. Hal and Grace started talking again; nobody else understood what they had been through. After extensive counseling, both separately and together, they found a way back.

Hal found a job with the Astoria PD; lower rank, less pay. But the job clicked with Hal and it turned out that the town of Astoria was a kind of salvation. Astoria was slower, simpler. Grace got a state job in Astoria. She hadn't worked out of the house since the boys were born. She enjoyed the job, her co-workers and even the walk to work. Grace worked in the blue State office building alongside the Riverwalk. The view from her desk, looking out at the Columbia River, was amazing.

Then they heard from Hal Jr. He lived in Kalispell, MT, with a girlfriend. He was a medic on the country's ambulance service and was looking to get on with the Kalispell Fire Department. When his girlfriend became his fiancé, Hal and Grace drove to Montana for the wedding. A year later, they had a grandson. Hal Jr. and his wife had thought of naming him Samuel, but it would have been too much. The grandson's name is Jesse.

Cherry didn't know any of this the night she drove Hal home. She found out, bits and pieces, over time. Some from Hal, some from Grace and more from a co-worker who had been with Portland PD when Hal was there.

Cherry and Grace didn't become friends; there was always a distance there. But they did respect one another and knew that they had a responsibility to Hal, to watch out for him on that terrible Anniversary.

32

CHARLIE COULDN'T REMEMBER that last time he'd asked a woman for a proper first date. A first date for Charlie usually meant a boozy roll in the hay after shots at a bar. The attraction depended on liquor and lust in equal amounts.

Dylan's lyrics 'love hits me first from down below,' summed it up.

With more than a little trepidation, Charlie approached the reception at Steak Deluxe!

"Hi Cassi, can I invite you to breakfast, maybe brunch this coming Saturday morning."

Jeesus, why am I so nervous? Charlie began to sweat.

"Well, which is it, Charlie"?

"Which is what?"

"Are you inviting me to breakfast or brunch?"

"Gee I'm thinking . . . brunch . . . . maybe late breakfast."

It came out more a question than a statement, but Cassi let it pass. She was enjoying the interchange.

"Charlie, will this be a Bloody Mary fueled bash, with the usual suspects from work?"

"No, no, just you and I. We both need a break from those knuckle-heads."

"What time?"

"What time what?"

"What time will you be picking me up for our date for brunch on Saturday?"

He's cute when he gets flustered like this, she thought.

"11, OK?"

"That would be perfect, Charlie. I'll be looking forward to it".

She bent down to get a couple of tissues from the Kleenex box under the counter.

"Here you go, Charlie. You're sweating into your collar just a bit."

I am soooo glad that's over, Charlie thought.

I haven't had that much fun in a long time, Cassi thought.

Saturday came bright, with blue skies and no wind. Charlie chose the Bistro on 11th; he'd heard they had the best Eggs Benedict in town. They sat at a sidewalk table. Cassi looked as bright as the day. Charlie felt glad he'd done this. Felt good about himself for the first time in a long time.

"You're not going to check their ticket times during our brunch are you Charlie?"

"No, of course not." He'd been doing just that.

"Good, let's get to know each other a bit."

No, no, we're not gonna talk feelings, are we? Please not that.

"Charlie, tell me what you worry about?"

"Well . . . . there is a thumping under the floorboards in my bedroom late at night."

"Thank you, Charlie. Tell me what worries you or I'll start talking about how important feelings are in a relationship."

Charlie told her his worries and a lot more.

They both ordered *'eggs benny and mimosas.'* They loved the eggs; the mimosas were so good they had another.

The Bistro got busy as the tourist crowd moved in.

"Thanks for brunch, Charlie; I could use some coffee to sober up. Can I buy you a cup?"

They walked down Commercial Street, talking, browsing at the store windows. Cassi wanted to show him a painting she liked at the RiverSea Gallery. Charlie liked it too, but the $3,000 price tag did give him pause.

"Who has 3-grand for a painting?"

"Those not in the service business Charlie."

They sat outside on picnic tables drinking coffee at the other Bistro, the one at 14th & Commercial.

"Why so many places in Astoria named Bistro?"

162

"Don't know. There's another one under the bridge in the Red Building."

"Charlie, I'm having a marvelous time."

"Me too."

33

AND SO, IT BEGAN. Cassi and Charlie became an item. They spent more and more time together off work. On the job, they remained professional with no sign of a personal relationship. But of course, everybody knew, it was obvious. Because of the good feelings they had for both Cassi and Charlie, the staff at the restaurant gave them a pass. No jokes, gossip, snickering, just left them alone.

Cassi got Charlie to give up his habit of being the last guy to leave work. He started trading off with Bill or

Ernie to do lights out and lock up. On the nights he didn't have the duty, Charlie let Cassi leave work first and wait in his car. Then Charlie would slip away. The charade fooled no one.

They usually stopped at Blaylock's Whiskey Bar. The dark, masculine space is a perfect spot for a late-night lover's rendezvous. Charlie & Cassi were drinking their way through the 180 whiskeys on Blaylock's list. After a couple of drinks, Charlie would drop Cassi off at her house. Sometimes he would come in for a cup of tea, but he didn't stay long. There was an unspoken agreement; they will take their time. The relationship is that important.

"So, Corey, where were we?" He is the couple's favorite bartender.

"Hey Charlie, hey Cassi." They slid into their favorite chairs at the bar. Baylock's has a program that tracked a drinker's progress through the Whiskey List.

"Well Charlie, let's see, according to our record, you had Johnnie Walker Black 2 nights ago, now you should be moving on to Ballantine's. You have 161 left to go."

"OK, give us 2 Ballantine's, neat."

"You know Charlie; we don't have to go at this like it's our job."

"Wouldn't it be nice if it was?"

2 whiskey's later, Charlie dropped Cassi off at her front door.

"Want to come in?"

"I should hit the road. It's late."

"I know it is and that's why you should come in. It would be wonderful if you could stay."

And it was . . . . wonderful.

34

THE APPLICANT FOR THE POSITION of Sous Chef came from an iconic high-end restaurant in Seattle. He would replace the former Steak Deluxe! Sous Chef, who is on his 3rd try at rehab. There had been quite a bit of back and forth between the applicant and the Chef.

Chef would make the hiring decision but Charlie would have input.

"I like the guy Charlie. I've asked around; he has a good rep."

"OK, but why is he leaving Seattle for here?"

"I think it's an opioid problem. But I checked around Seattle, no complaints and the place he's working at now gave him a good reference."

"Maybe they want to get a problem out of the way fast."

"Listen Charlie; we'll have him down; see how he cooks and go from there."

"Sounds like we're trading one druggy for another."

Chef didn't reply.

Bill, the applicant for the Sous Chef position, in other words, the Chef's right-hand man in the kitchen, arrived on a wet and stormy Astoria afternoon.

"Chef, I'm glad he's coming from Seattle, if it were Scottsdale he'd be leaving right after he said hello."

"Charlie, I can't figure out why I'm not living in Scottsdale."

They took Bill to the kitchen; after 90 minutes of hard questions and mostly true answers, the Chef asked him to cook for them.

"Make us an omelet," the Chef said.

As Bill got eggs, a pan and a whisk, Charlie asked Chef,

"Why an omelet? It's not even on the menu."

"It's what I want to see first. If the guy can't do that right, I don't care about anything else he cooks."

The omelet was served. "OK, that wasn't half bad." A high compliment from the Chef.

"Next, I'll call out a few things from the menu, you grab the ingredients and we'll see how you do."

"OK."

"After that, we'll set up for dinner service and at service, you'll work the line. I want to see how you are under pressure, how you are with the crew, how clean you cook."

'Cooking clean' is how a station looks during the shift. Is it a mess of bar towels, scraps of food, knives and other utensils not clean or not put back in place? A home cook could get away with this, especially if they have an understanding spouse. But in a commercial kitchen, it is a deal-breaker.

> "Tomorrow, Bill, we can go over my recipes and procedures at Steak Deluxe!"

Bill had driven 3 hours through a biblical storm to get to Astoria. He thought the afternoon would be a meet and greet; with the interview the next day. Now it looked like a 12-hour workday.

> "Chef, we need to set aside time to discuss my salary and__."

Charlie rolled his eyes at that remark.

> "We'll talk about that when and if I decide I want you. You need to show me what you've got first. This is an enormous opportunity for you. Prove to me that you deserve it." That was the Chef's reply.

Charlie thought,

'I'm still waiting for my enormous opportunity to work out.'

Steak Deluxe!

Dinner service went well for Bill. After a week of
protracted negotiations over the phone, he was hired
and came to work at Steak Deluxe!

35

THREE WAITRESSES HAD a post-dinner service drink at the Portway. Conversation turned to Bill, the new Sous Chef.

"Bill seems nice. Single too."

"He's not bad looking, I don't think."

"Huh?"

"Are you kidding me, his head looks like a taxicab with both doors open."

"His ears are kind'a big."

"Kind'a big? They're kind'a huge."

"I still think he's nice and nice looking."

"Thank you, Daisy-Mae."

"OK, what do you think, do-able?"

"Sure."

"Me too, what about you?"

"Maybe, if I keep my eyes closed tight and don't think about taxi's."

36

CHIEF OF POLICE SAM JACOBS likes things calm and
orderly. Astoria is a nice quiet town; Chief Jacobs saw
his job description as keeping it that way. Sure, there
would be disruptions. That came with the job, but it
didn't mean the Chief had to like them.

The biggest disruptions to Chief Jacobs sense of order
were the disappearance of the long time City
Councilman and the murder at Steak Deluxe!

First, the Councilman; Chief Jacobs, didn't like the
slimy bastard. Didn't like him from the first moment of

meeting; it went straight down-hill from there. Calm and order came from citizens who were straight shooters. Nothing about the Councilman was straightforward. When he talked, you knew he wasn't truthful and he knew that you knew he didn't care. The lie just lay there like a turd in the punch bowl. Chief Evans wasn't sure about the Councilman's wife either. She is truthful enough and damn good looking, but Chief Jacobs couldn't understand what on earth she saw in that sleaze-ball.

And now the murder at Steak Deluxe! The Chief of Police and his wife ate at Steak Deluxe! a couple of times a month. The Chef, who everyone in town knew as a tyrant, turned on the charm for Police Chief Jacobs and his wife. Sam Jacobs hated charm. But the food is good, the drinks generous. Even with that, the Chief knew something was off here. Couldn't put his finger on it, but something off-kilter.

Chief Jacobs did straighten one issue out after dinner at Steak Deluxe!

> "Chief Jacobs, Mrs. Jacobs, glad you could join us tonight. I hope you enjoyed your dinner."

> "Dinner was great. Thank you, Chef."

> "It's on the house, my compliments!" This is
the 3rd time the Chef offered.

"As I said before, I'll pay for our dinner. And I don't see it as a compliment; I see it as a bribe. If someone from my department eats here for free, I'll fire them and arrest you for attempting to bribe a law enforcement official. Do you understand?"

"Understood. Good evening."

Good evening my ass! I'd like to punch the sonabitch in the mouth, Chief Jacobs thought to himself.

37

NO ONE WAS SURE how Marty's murder would affect the restaurant's business. The Chef, Charlie (who was the new bookkeeper in addition to the rest of his duties) and everyone else thought things would turn out badly.

They were wrong, business boomed. The place packed every night. It seemed people came to dine and hoped for another killing just before dessert. As if Steak Deluxe! is a theme restaurant, with murder as the theme.

Another effect at Steak Deluxe! from Marty's murder is on the Chef. He started drinking more. Most people didn't think that was possible.

Chef had a shot of whiskey in the morning after coffee, just to get things going. Wine at lunch, a cocktail, or 3 before dinner service and a coffee cup of vodka next to his station during service. After closing, a drink with one of the kitchen staff who pissed him off the least. Then drinks at the bar with Charlie and the Chef's girlfriend of the moment. After that, a stop or 2 at a competitor's kitchen, to check on latest restaurant gossip, drinks there and usually a stop at Dirty Dan's for a quick one. Luckily, bars closed early in Astoria; Chef was in bed before 1am, on a good night.

His 2 main food groups were vodka & wine.

The Chef's kidneys used to hate him; now they wanted to kill him.

38

LUNCH RUSH IS OVER; dinner prep wouldn't start for a while. The new Sous Chef, Bill, joined Charlie and Bernie in the bar for a coffee break. These 3 are just about the only employees who don't smoke. It seemed silly to stand out in the rain with smokers just to get the latest gossip. They would get it soon enough and stay dry.

"Hey Bernie, give me a shot of rum in this coffee." Being a non-smoker didn't mean Bill is a non-drinker.

"Thanks." Bill took a sip, "much better. Well, it happened again last night and then again today during lunch service."

"What happened?"

"Chef went ape-shit on the entire kitchen."

Bernie had heard it before, had experienced it himself. He went back to inventorying the liquor bottles. It's Charlie's job to buck up new employees regarding Chef's bad behavior.

"Just shake it off, Bill. Talk to the most demoralized guys and get them back in the game. It'll be a different group every day. The Chef is an equal opportunity abuser."

"I don't know how you keep kitchen staff."

"Well, I'm not sure either, but we do. We pay them well and treat them like crap. It's an unusual human resource plan, but it's our plan, we're sticking to it."

Charlie continued,

"Here's another thing to know about the Chef. He's consistent. Every day he's gonna be an ass to somebody or more likely everybody. Get used to it or get out."

"But you seem to be the exception, Charlie. How come?"

"Don't know. There is a redeeming thing about the Chef, maybe the only one."

"What?"

"He needs to feed people. We took over weekend lunches for the Alternative High School here in Astoria. Just for a couple of months. A local church was doing it."

"This was the Chef's idea?"

"Totally. Kids went from peanut butter & jelly to steak sandwiches with crab-cake starters; it got out of hand. Prime rib and all the fixings one week. I had to beg the church to take it over again."

Bill appreciated Charlie's talk, but it was hard to believe the Chef was anything but the world's worst employer and biggest ass.

Charlie knew he'd have the same talk with Bill again.

A homeless guy wandered into the kitchen as dinner rush was slowing down. The guy tried to grab food out of pans, knocked into a couple of runners, finally just stood there looking at all the food. It seemed like he was at Disneyland.

Bill took off his apron, pushing the man towards the back door. He stopped when he heard the Chef;

> "Hang on Bill, bring him over here. The rest of you stop staring, start breaking down and cleaning up. I want this place sparkling, dammit."

Bill got a stool, left the man sitting in front of the Chef, the man's smell, over-powering.

Chef started cooking, bacon and eggs first. They went down fast, after that a small steak. Maylen brought over a cupcake and a slice of pie.

> "Juan, get me 6 to-go cartons."

> "Yes, Chef."

The Chef went around the kitchen, grabbing ingredients, shouting at line cooks, telling them how he wanted items cooked. Cooks brought him the finished entrees. The Chef inspected each one, putting the ones he approved of into a carton. He sent 2 back to be re-made.

The homeless guy wandered out the same way he came in, carrying 2 large sacks of food.

Bill and the rest of the kitchen staff watched all of this in wonder. *Maybe Charlie is right,* but Bill still had doubts, a lot of doubts.

39

THE CHEF AND BILL, the new Sous Chef, sat at the
Big O Saloon, in Olney, 12 miles south-east of Astoria.
Big O is part of a single business; gas station, grocery
store, bar/restaurant and community center for the
village of Olney. It has been the heart of the Olney
community since the 1890's.

The Klaskanine River was the only access to Olney in
those days, the store located beside it. When the
county built a road from Astoria to Olney, the store

was raised and moved a mile north to the new route. In any retail endeavor, it's always about location.

"Chef, we got a problem."

"No, Bill, you're just 2 weeks on the job; we don't have a problem, <u>you</u> must have a problem. And you drug me out to this place in the middle of nowhere. Does your problem have to be discussed in secret? How'd you even find this place?"

"Been in town for 2 weeks and I already know, everybody knows about the Big O. Surprised you don't Chef."

"Beginning to think my problem might be the smart-ass Sous Chef I brought on. I do like this place though. 1 waiter, 1 cook; efficient. Nice outdoor space. Great bar, wood stove."

"Glad you like it, Chef. I wanted to get you away from Steak Deluxe! to let you know about a situation in the kitchen."

"<u>My</u> kitchen."

"The problem affects you, me and everybody else working in that kitchen. You know who I'm talking about, you know he's been trouble long before I got here."

"Sid's been with us since the beginning." Chef is getting worked up.

"And he's probably been gumming up your kitchen from the beginning. On the line, Sid's slow, sloppy and a prick to everybody he works with."

"Wait a minute, Bill. I don't see any of that. Maybe a little slow . . ."

"When you're there, he's a marginal line cook. If you're not there, he's a minus, not a plus. Takes every short cut he can, doesn't follow your recipes."

"What'd you mean, doesn't follow my recipes?"

"Just that, leaves stuff out, adds different ingredients, brags about it."

"He's a little jealous he didn't get your job, Bill."

"Sid isn't qualified to be a Sous Chef at Steak Deluxe! or anyplace else. Staff is convinced the only reason he's in the kitchen now is how he sucks up to you."

In a rare moment of clarity and self-reflection, the Chef thought about Bill's points. Maybe Bill was right.

"OK, I heard you out. Now be sure and do your job right."

"I just did."

That's when things started to change in the kitchen at Steak Deluxe! The staff went from waiting to be the next one fired to being part of a skilled team. Sid was gone in a week; Bill became leader of the kitchen.

The Chef was still the boss, but Bill, the leader.

4:45pm. Kitchen and staff ready for dinner service.

The Chef isn't working this night. He took an additional day off to recover from a titanic hang-over that would have killed an amateur drinker.

Bill speaking to the kitchen crew, his crew;

> "OK, here's what we're gonna do. Everybody who comes into Steak Deluxe! our restaurant, gets a handcrafted, artisanal plate of love. Are you with me?"
>
> "Yes, Chef."

40

"Charlie, are you inviting me to meet your parents? Wow, that's a big step!"

Charlie hadn't realized it as a big step until right now. It made him nervous.

"Where do they live?

"Milwaukee."

"Oregon?"

"No, Wisconsin."

"Charlie, you're flying me to Wisconsin to meet your parents. I'm flattered; I'll have to buy a new dress, maybe new shoes from Gimre's."

He thought it was a good idea, yesterday. Now Charlie isn't sure if he'd thought it all the way through. He's sweating again; he can feel it running down his neck.

"Will they like me, Charlie?"

"Of course, they'll like you Cassi; everybody likes you."

"You say the sweetest things sometimes. I'm really looking forward to this. Thank you."

She said this as she handed him a couple of tissues.

"Maybe you should carry a pack of these in your pocket."

Charlie did the trip right. Instead of staying at a Portland airport hotel (you did that if you were on a business trip, this trip is pleasure), he and Cassi spent the night in a suite at the Marriott downtown. Drinks at the Heathman that night, then up Broadway to Higgins for dinner. Late-night Spanish coffee at Huber's.

Staying downtown meant an early wake-up for their 6:55am flight at PDX. Charlie left his car in the hotel garage; they took a limo to the airport. They arrived barely awake at 5:15. Early in the morning, PDX is a different place than later in the day. Travelers are experienced; know which lines to get in, what garments to take off, they are mostly businesspeople taking the first flight out, so they get in a full day's work at their destination.

On the plane, Charlie took the middle seat. *He is getting this gentleman thing down right,* thought Cassi. She fell asleep on his shoulder 10 minutes after takeoff, woke up on their descent into Milwaukee. At Cassi's insistence, they checked into their hotel room early; it cost Charlie an extra $75.

> "I'm not showing up at your parents, looking like a dog that's been left out over-night."

It took Charlie 20 minutes to unpack, wash-up and get ready to go. It took Cassi 2 hours.

They went past Charlie's grade school on the cab ride over to his parent's house. The neighborhood is small post-war homes; 2 stories, small lots, tiny front yards, a bit bigger backyards. Towering oak trees lined both sides of narrow streets, roots pushing up sidewalks. Beautiful trees, green leaves in summer, brilliant colors when leaves changed in the fall, then a big mess to clean up just before the snow started.

Charlie's Mother is at the door as they walk up the narrow path to the grey house with white trim and dormer windows.

"Charlie, Charlie . . . ." she hugged her son.

"Mom, this is Cassi." Charlie had spent the flight thinking of how he should introduce Cassi. *My friend, my girlfriend, my co-worker, my employee;* none of them sounded right, especially the last one.

"Welcome to our home Cassi; I'm June. Please come in." In her mid-70's, Charlie's Mom is slight and short, with grey hair, turning to white, sometimes blue, depending on her hairdresser. She sees her hairdresser every week.

The living room is small, made smaller by a stairway leading upstairs and a massive recliner. This chair is the kind of peculiar male furniture that includes cup holders, massage option, USB ports, possibly a small refrigerator and maybe a toilet, hard to know.

Swallowed up in all this is Charlie's Dad, Max.

"Max, dear, here's Charlie." Max is smaller than his wife, his hearing almost gone, his hair right behind.

"Who?"

"It's me, Charlie."

"Charlie, where?"

"Right here, Dad." Charlie pulled up a chair from the dining room table and sat next to his Dad. Held his hand.

Cassi and June sat on the small couch. There is Midwestern small-talk, weather, doings in the neighborhood, getting to know Cassi, catching up with Charlie. He is different around his parents, more outgoing, less negative. Like a burden lifted.

Max didn't say much, mostly responded to questions June would ask. Difficult to know how much Max understood.

Like Cassi, June knew what a big deal this was for her son. She wondered if he knew. June smiled as she watched the 2 of them together. She wasn't introduced to any of Charlie's girlfriends and hadn't met 2 of his wives until after they were married. The 3rd she never met.

"Gracious, where are my manners? Cassi, can I get you something to drink, maybe some tea?"

"Tea would be great, thank you."

"Charlie, how about you?"

"A Coke, please."

"I don't have Coke, is a Tab alright?"

"Sure Mom, thanks." *A Tab? Did they still make that? How old is this Tab I'm getting?*

June served crust-less egg-salad sandwiches as a snack. Max ate in his chair. After eating, Max became restless. The 2-extra people in his tightly held world bothered him; he got a little grumpy.

"Now Max, don't be cross."

His dementia is getting worse. Frustrated, cranky and sometimes angry, he can be a handful for his wife. The only way she can calm him works every time.

"Shush, now dear. The Packers are in the Super Bowl."

"Right, right . . . . . when is Super Bowl?"

"Today, it's just about to start. I'll make you some popcorn."

"Can I have a beer?"

"Sure, root beer."

"I don't want root beer; I want real beer. Real beer."

"Honey, let's not argue, the game is about to start."

"Right, right . . . . Super Bowl, popcorn, root beer."

"Coming right up!"

Her husband was born in Milwaukee, a life-long Packer fan. Years ago, he bought a VCR and taped every Packer game. Years and years of Packer games.

Now, going deeper into dementia, he watched a Packer game almost every day. Sometimes it was the Packer's season starter in 1983. The next day it might be Super Bowl in 2011 against the Steelers. He seemed to enjoy the 1997 Super Bowl the most. The Packers beat New England, 35 to 21; Max hated the Patriots.

Every day, every Packer game; brand new to him.

"Charlie, watch the game with your Dad."

"Yes, Ma'am."

41

THE 2 MEN SEQUESTERED in the living room with the Packer game, June and Cassi sat at the kitchen table talking. They talked about small things first and then about Cassi's job, her family, Astoria, Charlie and Max.

> "His dementia came on strong about 3 years ago. Before that, I didn't notice it much. He started losing keys, getting angry at little things, but it came to the point I couldn't

ignore it any longer. Our friends saw it first for what it was."

Cassi listened to June thoughtfully.

"The doctors are helpful. They prescribed Max meds; he takes a handful of pills every day. But Packer games work the best."

"Do you like football, June?"

"Hate it. His disease is like the end of the day, the sun is setting and my Max is in the twilight now."

"I'm so sorry."

"Thank you. It takes a lot out of a person." June was speaking about herself.

"Young and healthy, Max was a lot of fun. Bright, funny, very smart; he didn't go to college but he did read everything he could get his hands on.

"He worked at the Ford plant here for 32 years. That's a long time on the line. That work is hard on the body. Max didn't have the drive that Charlie has. Not sure where Charlie gets that from.

"Max loved Charlie from the get-go; almost worshiped him. Sure did love him. One time, when Charlie was a toddler and misbehaving, he started throwing food at me. I told him to stop, told him again, then I took him out of the highchair and put him on a time-out in the playpen in the living room. That kid screamed like a wild Indian.

"Of course, that's when Max gets home. He goes to see Charlie and he starts to pick him up.

"No, you don't, I said. You leave him right there! Max didn't dare pick him up. Charlie kept screaming; I kept looking at Max. He could tell I meant business.

"Max got between a rock and a hard place; I was the rock. But love finds a way. I went back to making dinner. When it got quiet in the living room, I went to see what was going on. Max had climbed into the playpen with Charlie."

Conversation turned to Cassi. Like Charlie, she was an only child. Maybe she grew up spoiled. She didn't think so but her friends sure did. Cassi's family went on a yearly vacation, someplace any Kansas kid would consider extravagant. One year it might be Disneyland, the next year Hawaii! Her mother was a schoolteacher, her father, an executive with a Kansas bank. When Cassi was in college, her parents died in a head-on crash on the highway outside of Topeka.

"June, my parents provided for me well, I have a trust fund. It's the kind of people they were. After the accident, I dropped out of KU for a year and lived with my Aunt. When it came time, my Aunt showed me some tough love and kicked me out the door. I went back to school and graduated."

"How did you get to Astoria?" June asked.

"Men, both stinkers. I met the first one in college, I thought he was the one. He decided I wasn't . . . . on our wedding day. I got stood up at the altar! My aunt would still like to kill him.

"The other one was nicer but I never thought he was it; more of a rebound thing. By then, I'd graduated with a degree in Art and taught in Lawrence at a junior-high school. He was a math teacher. We lived together for a while, always a bad idea. When we broke up, I looked at a US map and landed on Oregon.

"I sent out a bunch of resumes and got an offer in Astoria at John Jacob Astor elementary school. I run the Art program there and work at Steak Deluxe! in the evenings."

"A big move, Cassi. I'm glad it worked out for you."

"I researched it pretty well. I love the town, both my jobs, wouldn't have met Charlie otherwise. My big news this year is I bought a house, paid cash. No more rent checks."

"That's very impressive." June was getting to like this woman, a lot.

"It's what you can do, June, when you're a trust fund kid and work 2 jobs."

They talked a bit more, made dinner together for the boys. When Charlie and Cassi left that night, June said a prayer for her son;

"Dear Lord, don't let him screw this one up."

The kids (it's what parents call children of any age) stayed for another 2 days. Most of the time was spent in the house or outside in the backyard. It was hard to do more with Max. Cassi did take June shopping the 2nd day.

"We'll go to Nordstrom. A little retail therapy will be good for you, June."

Cassi told Charlie she'd like to buy June something, maybe a blouse or sweater. Charlie gave her $50 to help with the purchase.

"When was the last time you sent your Mother a gift on her birthday?"

Maybe once in the last 10 years, Charlie thought. He gave Cassi another $50.

While June was browsing in the Nordstrom shoe department, Cassi snuck off and found a beautiful sweater for June. She added $65 of her own money for the gift and had the salesperson wrap it while they had lunch.

Cassi had Charlie give his Mom the gift that afternoon but June knew who was behind it. June seemed a little cross with the 2 for spending money on her. But she wore it at the dinner table that night, with her apron on so there wouldn't be any spills. It seemed she might sleep in it.

The next day Charlie and Cassi stopped to say good-bye to June and Max on their way to the airport. June watched them drive away in the cab, then turned and went back inside to care for Max.

42

CHARLIE HAD NEVER SEEN the Chef look this bad
and that was saying a lot. The bags under his
permanently blood-shot eyes were huge. His pale skin
had taken on a near-death tinge. Every morning, he
had to double fist the 1st cup of coffee. A shot of
whiskey calmed the shakes. On some mornings, he
had the whiskey first, then coffee.

Staff couldn't figure the Chef out; one day he'd be
way up, business being great. Next day, Chef looked
like a man deep into grief for his favorite employee,

Marty. But that wasn't it at all. The Chef was scared shit-less. Sure, he liked the little guy, sent flowers to the funeral he didn't attend, but he was in trouble now. Chef had been in trouble all his life, but this was big and getting bigger every minute.

The Chef's finances were something nobody understood. When he bought Steak Deluxe! from what remained of Pan-Asian, he put together a small investor group, but it wasn't enough. He had to borrow big from a bank in Warrenton. When the loan became delinquent, the bank called it in. Frantic, Chef looked to his investors, but the response was negative. At the very last minute, Chef found his savior.

Axel Ace is a 40-year-old Finn from a long-standing Astorian family. A successful fisherman, he also owned a custom fish processing plant on the Astoria waterfront. Axel was successful but his need to present an uber-successful lifestyle (huge truck, Mercedes for the wife, Corvette for himself, big house on the hill in Astoria, condo in Palm Springs, condo in Hawaii and all of the rest of it) required a huge stream of cash. That's when Axel got into the drug business.

The fish and drug business.

Ace Fisheries sold the very best seafood, at the highest prices, to restaurants around the United

States, including Steak Deluxe! in Astoria. Clientele stayed small because of the expensive product. In spring, Axel sold Columbia River Spring Salmon, in summer Columbia Sturgeon, later in the summer Chinook Salmon – caught in the Columbia, Young's Bay or the Pacific Ocean close to shore. In early fall, the catch was tuna, caught 30 to 50 miles in the Pacific, west of the Columbia River mouth. Axel tried crabbing but it didn't fit his new business model.

Axel would make a yearly swing through the US visiting his accounts. Handshakes all around, informal chat with wait staff, another with kitchen crew, dinner with the chef and/or owner. The dinners were long, multi-course affairs, with the finest wines.
Somewhere along the line, cocaine came into the mix. Axel hadn't tried it before, but just to be polite, he tried it and liked it.

Liked it a lot.

43

"Good shit – don't you think?"

"Yeah man, thanks."

Lines of cocaine stretched out on an antique mirror, sitting on top of a butcher block in a deserted restaurant kitchen. Almost the size of a regulation basketball court, the kitchen had stainless steel everywhere. Axel and the Los Angeles chef/owner of the award-winning restaurant were the only people there. Alongside the mirror sat an unnecessary bottle of 25-year-old single malt scotch, 2 glasses. The dinner prior had lasted 2 hours.

"So, what were we talking about?"

"Can't remember."

"Me either. Want another line?"

"Sure."

The $350 Japanese knife made a delicate chipping sound as it minced through the coke on top of the mirror.

"I remember now; I was bitching about going to Sunset every time I run out of blow. I can get it from the dishwashers here, but then they think it's OK to use on the job. Half the time, you can't get into the staff john cause somebody's in there doing a line on top of the toilet tank."

The owner/chef had scarfed a long line of the drug, half in one nostril, half in the other.

Axel, drunk first, wired now, with a million things flashing through his brain, had only one rational thought, *'don't do any more blow.'* But he did anyway.

"It's a drag; I'm worried a customer will see me buying on the Strip." The Chef/owner again.

"Come on; you can get a guy that'd bring it here to the restaurant or your house." Axel felt his jaws tighten from the coke.

"Yeah, the house, my wife catches me with drugs; it's not my house anymore. I swore to her I'd stop. Plus, it's expensive that way. As much as I use, I need a wholesale price."

It took a while for Axel to respond. He had to get his thoughts in line.

"I could help you out. Mike at (he named a high priced, modern Italian bistro in Seattle) knows a guy, deep into coke, who's looking to broaden his business."

"Great, let me know. I appreciate it. You want any more of this?"

"Good God no . . . . sorry. No, thanks."

Axel heard the click, click, click as he walked out the door, trying to remember where he parked the rental car.

That's how Ace Fisheries' side business started. In less than a year, it was the business. Fish became a sideline.

Axel owned 2 boats and he bought fish from other local boats. Iced fish moved from the boats to the processing plant via a crane on the plant's wooden outdoor deck and then were wheeled inside. On long stainless-steel tables, the fish were gutted, cleaned, beheaded. The next step; putting the fish into 4-foot long, strong, waxed cardboard boxes, ice on top.

The step that Axel added was 1 kilo of cocaine in waterproof packaging placed in the belly cavity of each fish. Topped off with another layer of ice, the boxes sealed, labeled and shipped.

Every couple of weeks, an Ace Fisheries truck would leave Astoria for a 3-hour drive to Seattle, Axel at the wheel. The product, cocaine, loaded into the truck. 3 hours back to Astoria.

One of the problems this success caused Ace Fisheries was the amount of cash coming in. All shipments that contained fish and drugs had to be paid in cash prior to shipment. The difference in cash-flow before drugs and after drugs at Ace Fisheries was too big to avoid scrutiny from the IRS.

That's where Steak Deluxe! came in. Axel would run drug cash through Steak Deluxe! The Chef would take a percentage and the money would go back to Ace

Fisheries (less the percentage and additional skim Chef took off the top for himself) in the form of payments for bogus invoices.

This bit of bookkeeping was known only to the Chef. He handled it himself. His bookkeeper Marty didn't know about it, neither did his manager, Charlie.

Axel had gone into the fish/drug business and now the Chef was into the restaurant/money laundering business. These 2 business models worked great for a couple of years; then they didn't.

Didn't in a big way.

44

ACE FISHERIES HAD 15 ACCOUNTS that got a fish/cocaine shipment and 23 that received only fish. Axel worried that the loads would get mixed up, but it never happened.

Disaster came in a completely different way.

FedEx was delivering an overnight shipment from Ace Fisheries to a high-end restaurant in Boston. A shipment containing salmon and unknown to FedEx, cocaine. The van carrying the shipment from the Boston airport to a restaurant downtown was side-swiped by a commuter attempting to eat a bagel and text at the same time. He succeeded in this but failed when he added a café latte to the mix. It landed in his lap.

His car careened from the far-left lane into the middle lane, clipping the FedEx van's left-rear quarter panel. This sent the FedEx van directly in the path of a UPS van in the right lane. If there had been a US Postal vehicle involved, a rare trifecta of package delivery brand accidents could have been achieved.

Unfortunately, that wasn't the case. Impact with the UPS van caused the FedEx's rear door to explode open just as it began a sickening 180-degree slide, losing packages across all 3 lanes of freeway. It ended up with the rear-end facing forward.

After the collision with FedEx, the UPS van slammed into a showroom perfect 1964 Volkswagen Bug, scrunching it against a concrete barrier. The only thing keeping the Bug from falling 25 feet to the roadway below was the rusted metal railing on top of the barrier.

The middle lane turned into a daisy chain of smashed vehicles, starting with a Lexus SUV directly behind the FedEx van. The driver slammed on his brakes hard, lost control, fishtailing so that half of the SUV went into the right lane where it was smashed by a minivan. And the minivan, hit by another vehicle, and that vehicle, hit by another, and so on.

A long-distance trucker, carrying live chickens from rural Willimantic, Connecticut to Bangor, Maine tried to avoid all this mess, by maneuvering into the left lane. There the trucker met a Tesla sedan trying to get out of the same mess. Tesla is a fine car but in a demolition derby, it is not a real match for an 18-wheeler carrying chickens. After that crack-up, live chickens, dead chickens, feathers, packages everywhere.

Accident Report; 23 vehicles involved, no fatalities but plenty of scrapes, bruises and enough whiplash and emotional distress to keep a battalion of accident lawyers working for months. The freeway was closed for 14 hours.

During the cleanup, amidst the chickens, living and dead, were 3 large boxes of salmon. The boxes had burst open; all the fish had a package of cocaine inside.

The Massachusetts State Police got involved, then the DEA and then Axel Ace and Ace Fisheries were over. A great idea turned into a horrible one, in a New York minute on a Massachusetts freeway.

Axel Ace was sentenced for a long list of crimes that amounted to 9 years in prison. 4 Ace Fisheries employees were convicted for a shorter list and given 24 months.

One interesting aspect of a very interesting crime was that the only money recovered was found at Ace Fisheries and Axel's residence.

The link between Ace Fisheries and Steak Deluxe! was never discovered. The restaurant lost an essential source of income, the percentage earned from money laundering and the amount skimmed by Chef.

Chef needed to replace that lost income fast. He had no idea how.

45

IT WAS THE USUAL GROUP at the bar after closing; Chef, Bill, Charlie and Bernie, finishing up behind the bar. Tonight, the group included 2 regular customers, regular enough that they could stay after closing. The discussion, same as every night, women & sports, sports & women.

Chef heard knocking at the front door first.

"Bill, go see who it is."

Bill ambled off, came back with a stunning blonde beauty. Stunning enough for all 5 men at the bar to stand up.

Charlie had to smile; *a bar is always open for a good looking blonde.*

"Hi Charmaine, I'm just about done here." Unbelievably it was Bernie that spoke to the blonde goddess.

"Can I buy you a drink?" The 2 regulars and Bill said this in unison.

"Thank you but no, I'm taking Bernie to my place for a nightcap."

"I'm sorry honey, my manners, Charmaine, meet the guys. Guys this is Charmaine."

"Nice to meet you!" Again, in unison.

Bernie got his coat, clocked out, escorted his lady friend out the door.

There were several moments of stunned silence.

"What did I just witness?" One of the regulars.

"Seen it before, a bunch of times. Several different women." The Chef.

"I think the one before was better looking," Charlie said.

"Not possible to be <u>better</u> looking." The other regular.

"I disagree, the woman 3 women before this one was the best looking. So far." Chef again.

"So, what is it with Bernie? Nice guy but come on, not handsome, a car that doesn't run, a dump of an apartment and no money working for you Chef. What is it?"

The Chef took a long slug of vodka to clear his thoughts.

"I've thought about this a lot and here's the deal with our boy Bernie. When women talk to him, he listens. Doesn't correct them, doesn't try to solve their problems. Just listens."

The responses from the other men in the bar were remarkably similar.

"I gave up listening, 2 wives ago."

"No wonder I haven't had a date in 5 years."

46

"Chef, we need to increase the cash coming
out of this joint."

Chef had been thinking the same thing since Axel
went to jail. But he didn't want to hear about it from
these musclebound knuckleheads.

"Well let me think on it, I have a couple of
good ideas, I'll get back to you."

At least Chef sat behind his desk, in his own chair.
One Finn stood, taking up all the space in the Chef's

office and most of the oxygen. The other one stood in the hallway.

"We thought about it for you, Chef. We need some warehouse space and a little help with distribution."

"Distribution of what?"

"What's with the questions, Chef? We got a good plan, you're gonna help us."

"There's no room to warehouse anything here."

"It's a climate sensitive product. We're putting it in your locker, the one with the steaks."

"No way, the Steak Locker is just that, for steaks nothing else. What do you mean climate sensitive?"

"Again, Chef we have the__ "

"You guys are talking drugs, aren't you? Coke, is that it?"

"No not coke, it's all over the stree__"

"Heroin that's it, right? Right?"

The 2 giants didn't deny it.

The Chef moved directly from the frying pan, into the fire.

47

IT'S LATE, PAST 1AM. The Chef, past tired. He'd done both lunch and dinner services. Lost his temper numerous times at both. He knows everybody in the kitchen hates him but at least they fear him. The Chef isn't sure if that's better or worse.

The new Sous Chef, Bill, improved the kitchen at Steak Deluxe! The improvement pleased the Chef; he'd hired the right guy. It also pissed him off. The kitchen crew likes Bill, and more than that, they respect him. Nobody likes the Chef as far as he could tell. And there is a big difference between fear and respect.

> '*What am I, 6 years old? They like the new kid better than me? Why the hell do I care?*'

The Chef's thoughts came to him as he sat at his dining room table, the lights out. He lives in a modern condo in the east-end of Astoria with a great view of the Columbia. The inside of the condo looks like hell. At work, a tyrant regarding cleanliness; at home, he doesn't care.

That's the reason for lights out. Lights on, the disaster zone he calls home would be visible. The living room is a jumble of magazines, bottles (whiskey, vodka, wine, brandy and beer; all empty), stained carpet, dirty clothes, shoes (his own and 2 pair of high heels). Some woman left her bra on the floor beside the couch; another left her purse. The Chef could look inside and call the woman but it seems like too much effort. The awesome view that sold him on the place is behind curtains that are never opened. He hasn't set foot on the outside deck.

The condo has 2 bathrooms; one is the 'guest bathroom.' He never uses it. It's clean but without soap and towels. The other bathroom, off his bedroom, looks like a crime scene. The bedroom itself is terrifying, even to the Chef.

> *'I'm paying a $3-grand mortgage, $6-hundred*
> *in HOA fees, every damn month and it looks*
> *like I'm living at the dump.'*

The thought comes as the Chef pours a completely unnecessary slug of vodka into a dirty glass. He drinks it down and another thought comes, so unfamiliar it feels like a revelation.

> *'What am I doing? Is this me, to live like this . .*
> *. . to act like this? I've been going down his*
> *road so long it seems normal to me.'*

This is a rare and remarkable bit of self-reflection. In his life and work, the Chef comes off as a bully, a petty tyrant, wildly self-assured. He's OK with the image, but it's not true. Behind all that, the Chef is anxious, unsure. And he won't reveal this to anyone, even himself. That's what makes this alcohol-fueled séance so amazing. The Chef is admitting something big to himself. And it scares the shit out of him.

> *'Normal? This is normal? Not by a long shot.*
> *What is it with my drinking, how many drinks*
> *did I have today? 10 or 15? Hell, I had that*
> *many at work. After work, another 5 or 6, and*
> *I'm having another one now.'*

The Chef throws the last dregs of vodka and glass against the wall, followed by the bottle. His drinking had always influenced his life and now was hurting his work. Burns and cuts were part of a kitchen job, but lately, they were occurring more often to Chef. Yesterday, he burned his arm badly when a pan slipped out of his hand. Last week a gash in his thumb took 12 stitches to close. Most of the line cooks were faster than him. And they executed the Chef's recipes, more accurately than he did.

> 'And the women? I haven't had a relationship that lasted more than a couple of months. What am I looking for, what is it I can't find? I treated all of them like shit, even the ones I liked. Did I love any of them, don't think so?'

The Chef had tried AA 3 times, expensive rehabs twice. Didn't take, any of them.

> 'What now? Try all of that again? Waste more money? I had chances but I didn't try hard enough. And really didn't believe in any of it. This is my path and I'm staying on it. I'm an old dog, too old and tired, to take up new tricks.'

That last thought hit the Chef like a thunderbolt. It stopped him; he took it in, waited. And knew it was true.

It turns out there is a little vodka left in the bottle on the floor. The Chef chokes it down and heads to bed.

48

LORELL LEFT HER APARTMENT on Bond Street; it is her day off, she looked forward to her favorite Astoria pastime. She lives a few blocks from the Columbia River and the Riverwalk that parallels the River. A historic trolley runs down the middle of the Walk with bicycle and walking paths on each side. The sun is shining, wind light. The River, 4 miles wide at this point, roared past on its way to the Pacific, glistening like a brilliant blue ribbon.

A feeling of happiness and comfort swept over Lorell as she got to the Riverwalk. In her late 20's, with a good job, a great boyfriend, she is living in the right town at precisely the right time.

Lorell came to a faint trail that led down the 10-foot embankment from the Riverwalk to the Columbia River. She had checked her tide table and got to the River at morning low tide, lowest of the month. Water could come up high on the embankment during high tide, but now at low tide, the embankment was dry, water 30 yards out. An underwater landscape, rarely seen, revealed. Vibrantly green moss-covered rocks, the sun shining down on the rocks and water, the scene almost blinding.

And incredibly beautiful.

Head down, moving carefully, Lorell walked out on the rocks. Didn't walk as much as slipped and slid, lucky she didn't break an ankle on the mean, moss-covered rocks. She looked for opium bottles, dishware, anything interesting from the days when this was the shoreline for a bustling Astoria Chinatown. An interesting hobby for her, but not an income endeavor. But neither was golf, her other favorite hobby.

Chinatown and Chinese immigrants were the work-force engines that ran dozens of salmon canneries on Astoria's waterfront from the mid-1800's to the

1940's. Chinese labor also helped build the jetties at the mouth of the Columbia River, built the dikes that kept the Columbia out of downtown and were essential in getting the city sewer system built.

For Chinese immigrants, it was money for muscle. A lot of muscle; not much money and less respect.

Cannery workers worked 16-hour shifts and would often have to cut their rubber boots to release swollen feet at the end of the day.

Chinatown was a densely populated 6 square block area which started near the corner of 6th and Bond Streets. Chinatown was a separate town, apart from Astoria. Not much interaction between the 2 towns.

Chinatown had the stores and businesses any small-town would have; hardware, groceries, banks, doctors, dentists. And an abundant number of bars, tea shops, restaurants.

In addition, Chinatown had numerous card rooms, betting parlors and an equal number of whorehouses and opium dens.

Tongs became part of Chinatown starting in the 1870's; they grew to as many as 9 different Tongs. They ranged from criminal to social organizations. As time passed, the Tongs became known more for benevolence than violence. They began to disappear in the 1930's.

Little is left of Chinatown, just 1 building remains. The building had been a house of 'ill-repute' on the top floor, a restaurant on the street level, a gambling hall and opium den in the basement. Today the ground floor houses a Thai restaurant and a property management office.

Just the week before, Lorell had found an intact top half of a Chinese 'Tea Jar.' These Jars are highly decorated ceramic pots up to 18" high, 12" in diameter. They were used by Chinese sailors in the 1800's to hold a blend of tea leaves from their home province. The tea made from these leaves made a warm, welcome remembrance of home on long Pacific voyages. Being ceramic, 1 wave could bash a century-old Jar into pieces. It was unusual to find such a large undamaged piece.

Lorell rushed home, washed her treasure carefully. Lorell had found an article from centuries before and brought it back to life. It could be worth a lot of money, but Lorell didn't profit from her finds, just having them, enough for her.

This day Lorell scrambled across the rocks for a good hour without finding anything of interest. Then in about 3 feet of water, she saw a flash of something bright. Slowly she made her way to it and found a modern pistol, shiny barrel, with black cross-hatched handles. Lorell was afraid to touch it, but it was mesmerizing. After several minutes she decided to pick it up by the barrel. She didn't want to hold it anywhere near the trigger. *Is it loaded?* She didn't know how to check.

Just as she bent down, Miss Molly, the 26-foot power launch that serviced the ships at anchor with food, supplies and mail, roared by sending a big wake toward shore. The wake knocked Lorell back on her butt, she landed on a rock, trying to get off that, fell on her back into deeper water and went under holding the gun high.

It took her a good long time to get turned around and upright. 5 minutes to shore; afraid to fall, afraid to drop the gun, deathly afraid she'd shoot herself. Then up the embankment to the Riverwalk.

There Lorell stood; wet, cold, her calf-high rubber boots filled with river water, holding a gun. Her hair, dripping wet, coated with green river slime. A couple of workers in the office building on the other side of the Riverwalk called the police.

> "A crazy woman, she came out of the river, with a gun!"

Lorell had left her car at home. Just as well, she was too wet and dirty to get in a car. But she did need to get rid of the gun; she headed for the police station. As she walked, people jumped out of her way. A couple of cars jammed on their brakes; others stomped on the gas. Police sirens were all around her, but Lorell didn't hear any of it. She was on a mission to get rid of the damn gun, take off the damn boots. The squelching sound they made with every step, drove her nuts.

She took a short cut through the alley behind the flower store where her boyfriend worked. He happened to come out the back door of the store.

"Jeesus Lorell, it only happened once! It'll never happen again. Drop the gun."

"What?"

"Drop the gun." This time it didn't come from her boyfriend; it came from a cop at the end of the alley. "Drop the gun now." There it was again, this time from an officer at the other end of the alley. Both had pistols drawn, pointed at Lorell.

"I'm afraid if I drop it, it'll go off. Take the gun and help me get these damn boots off."

Astoria police officers took the gun and at the station helped her with the boots. Lorell appreciated the towels, blanket, coffee, but it did little to help her mood. After a lengthy and to Lorell's mind, unnecessary debriefing, her boyfriend drove her home.

Jim Hallaux

First, she stood in the shower until the hot water ran out. Then Lorell drank a mug of tea and followed that up with a shot of whiskey.

Then she looked her boyfriend dead in the eyes and asked,

"What only happened once?"

49

"Charlie, I have a question for you."

"Cassi, I didn't do it, wasn't even there."

"Don't get cute. I have a serious question but first, I have a reminder."

They were sitting at the Silver Salmon restaurant, in the back corner, surrounded by colorful artwork on the walls, most of it nautical, some hand-drawn on the white paper table coverings in the restaurant.

Each year Silver Salmon held a drawing for the best customer art. Charlie had submitted 2 entries and was a little miffed when Cassi suggested they looked like something a young child might draw. Cassi, the art major, submitted a crayon drawing she made while eating dinner one night, it was framed on the wall above them.

"OK, what's the reminder."

"The reminder, Charlie, is that if you order another steak at the Silver Salmon restaurant, I will have to get up and smack you." She said this with a smile and a wink.

"Violence is never the answer, Cassi."

"Well come on! There are about 5 different ways you can have salmon here. Order one. We work at a steak house, order salmon at Silver Salmon!"

"Got it, I got it. What was your question?" Charlie asked this to change the subject.

"Why have you buried yourself in work all these years? You've gotten better but I wonder how much of your life you've missed."

'I hate this kind of question,' Charlie thought to himself but knew he'd have to answer.

Charlie was saved by the waitress asking for their order. Cassi ordered chowder, salad and a smoked salmon entrée. Charlie ordered a hamburger and fries. The conversation during dinner was light, they talked about this and that, nothing about work and nothing too deep. Charlie hoped Cassi had forgotten the earlier topic.

It was a slow night at Silver Salmon; they could have the table for as long as they wanted. They asked for coffees and Sambuca.

"So, Charlie, back to my question. You're a lifer in the restaurant business I get that. But there's more to you than the job. Right?"

"OK, I'll admit I took my job way too seriously for a long time__."

"Now there's an understatement."

"If you'll let me continue. During that time, I let everything else go. Didn't pay much attention. Didn't pay attention to friends, relationships, wives, my health. Just let all that take care of itself. But now, all of that changed. I care now; it's like I woke up."

"What made you change, Charlie?" Cassi lowered her eyes, the slightest suggestion of a smile on her lips. "What changed you?"

"You did, Cassi, love of my life." He said it kiddingly, but it was true.

"Ah, Charlie, really? You say the sweetest things. So, tell me how long have you worked in restaurants?"

"Since I was 16, please don't do the math, it's a long time. Started in the dish pit. Then runner, host, waiter, I wasn't great at that. I started doing the schedule at a joint, that led me to running front of house, a couple of joints later I became an assistant manager, then manager and the rest is history."

"You are very good at your job."

"Thanks, but you're right, it comes at a cost. I guess what hooked me about this business first was being part of a team. You had to prove yourself and then you're in. And your life starts to revolve around the restaurant; all your friends are there, it's your job and social life wrapped into one. And it's fun, at least in the beginning. When it became a career . . . . not as much. But still fun. A bar manager once told me in this business you must join the party. It's a hard party to leave."

Cassi thought on that a bit.

"I'm surprised you didn't like being a waiter."

"Whoa, I didn't say that. I loved being a waiter, head up, eyes on my tables, controlling the flow of the dinners. And I loved having money in my pockets every night. It's just that I wasn't good at it. Too clumsy, too slow, too friendly. I can train a waiter; I just can't be a waiter.

"And now, Cassi, I'm too old to start over in a new career."

Their coffee cold and the Sambuca gone, Cassi and Charlie headed home to Cassi's house on the hill.

50

"Cherry, did you hear back from the State Police Lab in Salem?"

"About the gun in the river, Chief?"

"Yes, about the damn gun, what else do we have at the Salem lab?"

The Chief was getting a bit grumpy over the slow resolution to the murder at Steak Deluxe!

"I'll call them again right now."

"Tell them if we don't hear back this afternoon, I'm driving down to Salem myself. And they're not going to like it when I get there."

"Yes, sir."

The Chief stormed off.

Ballistic testing proved this was the gun used in the murder of Marty Klein, the bookkeeper at Steak Deluxe! The next thing to prove is the ownership of the weapon.

The serial number on the gun was partially etched out, making it impossible for Astoria PD to decipher. The lab in Salem used new technology recently purchased to reveal the numbers.

Late that afternoon, the State Lab identified the owner of the gun as a Hans Jhuta, a resident of Astoria. Once Astoria PD got the gun ID, a patrol car was dispatched and Hans Jhuta brought to the station. Cherry left him sitting alone in interview room #2. She let him stew for a while.

After 45 minutes, Cherry began the interview. In short order, she learned that Hans had lent the gun to his nephew for a 'little target practice' 2 years ago.

"I forgot all about that. Just last week I wondered where that damn gun went. Can I get it back?"

"No Hans, you can't get it back, its evidence in a murder investigation. And now I will read you your rights."

"My rights? Wait a minute, wait a minute; what do you want to know? I'll tell you, that kid was a squirrelly bastard from the get-go."

"Are you sure you don't want a lawyer?"

"No, I ain't mixed up in any murder."

Hans told Cherry everything she needed to know. She had the name and address of half of what appeared to be a 2-man crime syndicate. After further discussion, she had the other half.

Cherry needed to brief the Chief. She called him at home.

"I'm right in the middle of dinner, Cherry. Can I call you back?" Dinner was a sacred time at the Jacobs household.

"It can't wait Chief!"

The Chief listened as Cherry gave him the run-down.

"So, Cherry a 2-man crime spree?"

"Well, not really a spree, they've been at it for a while. I wouldn't call it 'organized crime', more of a chaotic, not so bright Mafia."

"The Mafia? La Cosa Nostra?. . . . . . in Astoria? Cherry, really?"

"No, not Italian . . . . a 2-man Finnish Mafia."

Both members of the Finnish Mafia had records for petty and fairly stupid crimes in and around Astoria. They were distant cousins and lived at the same address. A 103-year-old, 2 story house on Marine Drive in a neighborhood called Uniontown. It was a convenient location for them. 3 bars, 2 restaurants and a coffee shop all within stumbling distance of their residence. The Astoria–Megler Bridge soars above the area.

What would have been the front yard is used for parking. Between the 2 men were 5 vehicles, most of them drive-able. One cousin lived downstairs, the other upstairs.

On this night, the cousins weren't at home. They were having a 'come to Jesus' meeting with Chef. They barged into the kitchen at the end of dinner rush.

"Chef, we need to talk with you. Now."

"I can't, not for an hour, at least."

"We'll wait in the bar."

The Chef didn't want these 2 mastodons in his bar. Last time they were there, they left with an unpaid $300 bar bill.

> "Go outside; I'll be 5 minutes."

> "Outside, in the rain? In the parking lot?"

> "Yes, in the parking lot. Get out of my kitchen now, let me try and get these dinners out."

The 2 member Finnish Mafia marched out the back door, mumbling as they went.

> "What the hell got into him?"

> "Can I rough him up, just for fun?"

> "Maybe."

Chef came out with a drink in one hand, a cigarette in the other.

> "What is so damn important?"

> "What is so important is you having teeth in your mouth and 2 unbroken arms."

The Chef could see meeting them outside was a big mistake. He stood hemmed in by the dumpster and the 2 huge Finns. The parking lot; dark, deserted.

Maylen finished having a rare smoke break at the other end of the dumpster. She had just ground out her cigarette when the 2 huge men came out. She stood, silent, listening to them and the Chef.

> "We need more money out of this operation and we're gonna get it, starting now. We'll move the Steak Locker around, bring in the new product."

> "Heroin? No way."

The Chef said this as he raised the hand with the cup in it, vodka sloshing over his chef's jacket. He pointed his index finger at the larger of the 2 giants as if it was a gun. Right then, the Chef realized he was defenseless. What could he do, finger them to death?

> "We're done talking to you, Chef. We are telling you there will be new product in the Steak Locker. You either get on board or you are going overboard with a bullet through your head."

As he spoke, the giant pushed his index finger into Chef's sternum, hard. It felt like the finger was going through his body.

> *Lord, Lord, save me.*

> "So, what's it gonna be, Chef? In or out? I don't care; the new guy Bill can take over for you, at half of what you're making. My friend here wants to give you a beating for pleasure

before he puts a slug in your head and pitches you in the river."

Chef had trouble standing.

"Chef, Chef." Another stab to the sternum. "In or out? Yes or no."

"Yes," it came out as a whisper, almost a plea.

The 2 giants ambled off, Chef fled to the sanctuary of his office, closed the door, turned out the lights. He took a bottle of Vodka out of a drawer, drank from it. No glass.

Maylen watched the giants walk to their car at the other end of the parking lot. They stood there, smoking, talking. The Chef had stumbled back into the kitchen. After a minute, Maylen followed. She grabbed a long, slender boning knife at the Chef's station, found a sharping stone and a small bottle of mineral oil.

As she left the back door of the kitchen, Maylen saw the 2 men getting into their car. She got in her car and followed, not too closely; she knew where they were going.

The Mafia headed to Dirty Dan's. They parked in the gravel parking lot, had another smoke by the front door, entered the bar.

Maylen sat in her car, parked on the street, lights out. Calm, patient, mind turned off, sharpening the Chef's knife.

51

8PM THE SAME NIGHT.

Cherry sent a patrol car to the cousin's house on Marine Drive.

> "I want to know if they are home but I don't want them aware. Don't go to the door."

10 minutes later, the patrol radioed back.

> "No lights or movement in the house."

> "OK, check every bar in town. Let me know."

35 minutes later;

> "Found them at Dirty D's, Lieutenant. What now?"

> "Sit on the location, let me know when they leave and follow."

> "Got it. Out"

Midnight

The patrol officer sat in his cruiser, watching the door of Dirty D's. He gave up smoking 2 weeks before and eased nicotine withdrawals with an extra-large bag of peanuts and a thermos full of coffee. There would be hell to pay at the shift change. He'd have to vacuum out the cruiser; peanut shells were everywhere. If this was detective work, he'd stay with patrol. Just as he thought his bladder would explode, the 2 big men came out of the bar.

The patrol followed the cousins back to their house on Marine Drive. The officer kept going, made a U-turn, parked a block away with a good view of the front of the house. He watched the lights go on in the house, first downstairs, then upstairs.

He watched a car make an illegal U-turn, similar to his own. On a regular shift, he'd pull the driver over for a ticket.

"They're in their house Detective Johnson. What now?"

"Sit on it. I can't get a search warrant signed. There's a shindig at the Country Club; I can't get a Judge to call me back. Just let me know if they leave. We'll execute the warrant in the morning."

"Hey, my shift ended at midnight. Where is the replac___"

"You're all I've got. You stay there, stay awake. I'll be at the station; I need to set up the search team, could be a lot of weapons, State police might get involved."

'Isn't this special, another 6 hours in the car. No peanuts, no coffee, no life.' The patrolman muttered to himself.

Against his better judgment, the officer called his wife at 12:30am. Not a long call and not particularly pleasant. But he didn't want his wife to wake up in the morning with him not there. She'd probably appreciate the call more in the morning, or maybe not.

52

THE COUSINS LEFT THE DIRTY D BAR at midnight, headed home. Maylen follows, watches them park their car and enter the house. She makes a U-turn, turns right at the Doughboy Monument. Then up Alameda Avenue, until she sees the cousin's house below and parks her car. The night is silent; nobody out, no wind, no rain. Maylen heads down a pedestrian trail that leads past the cousin's backyard and on to Marine Drive.

Maylen moves casually, she's in no rush. Her stride is confident. As she slips through the dilapidated backyard fence, a neighbor's dog starts barking. The dog's owner comes to the back door to tell the damn dog to shut up. Maylen stops, waits. The chastened dog is let back inside. Maylen still waits. 5 minutes later, she moves to the back door of the cousin's house. The top half of the door is glass, covered inside with a dingy cloth curtain. She sees a light on and movement through the curtain. Maybe one of the giants is making a midnight snack.

What do they eat late at night? Large rodents? Maylen smiles to herself.

She bangs on the back door and shouts;

"HELP ME. HELP ME."

A giant figure fills the door, blocking out light from the kitchen. The door opens inwards.

"What the hell?" The cousin sees it's a woman, puts the gun he has in his hand down on the kitchen table. It's like he knows her or has seen her someplace.

"What'd you want? You scared the shit out of..."

The first 2 stabs go in the giant's ample gut, the next 2 to his chest, 1 directly into his heart, last 2 into his neck. He falls to his knees, then, with a soft moan, falls to the floor, blocking the doorway.

The body is dead, but the blood keeps flowing. Maylen has no choice but to climb over the massive, bloody corpse. She thinks about stabbing again but decides against it. An ammonia smell of blood fills the kitchen. There are 2 pools of blood, one on the back porch and one, on the other side of the body, on the kitchen floor. Both are growing bigger.

Maylen moves from the kitchen to the living room; it is as she expected. Horrid.

How do people live like this?

She hears someone moving upstairs, more like stumbling. Maylen goes to the bottom of the stairs. Between the foot of the stairs and front door is a small alcove. She waits there, doesn't hide, just waits. The other giant comes down the stairs, slowly, unsteady. He is wearing only a pair of massive boxer shorts that, in another lifetime, might have been white. His drunk cousin was the 'designated driver' tonight, so this cousin is much drunker.

As he steps off the stairs, Maylen slips the blade in just under his ribs, then sharply up. The giant puts his hands over the spurting wound with an astonished look on his face. Maylen is standing on the wrong side of him; she can't get to his heart; she goes for his neck. 3 stabs there. As he starts to go down, he turns to face her and exposes his heart. She stabs him there, several times.

The blood seems to turn the entire room red.

Maylen climbs over this monster and moves back through the living room. She notices figurines on the mantel above a fireplace that hasn't been cleaned in years. There is a pair of Paul Bunyan and Blue Ox salt/pepper shakers. Paul Bunyan stands on a pedestal that says 'Astoria'; Blue Ox has 'Oregon' across its side. Her hand wavers over the tourist souvenirs. She finally selects Blue Ox and puts it in her pocket. Maylen sees herself in a cracked mirror over the crumbling fireplace. There is blood in her hair, on her face; her white shirt is now mostly red. The check chef's pants wet, the Croc shoes she wears squishy with blood.

She looks like death walking, and she feels great.

Maylen goes back into the kitchen, climbs over the other monster, out the door and into the night.

The night is still calm and silent. As she walks up the trail, Maylen is intensely alive; renewed and glorious.

53

ASTORIA POLICE CHIEF JACOBS got to the station at 6am; Search Warrant signed at 7am. State Police wouldn't be involved but Clatsop County Sheriff's Deputies would be. Both departments synced up and ready to go. The patrol officer who watched the house overnight was relieved by another officer but he said he'd stay on site. He didn't want to miss the action.

The Chief, the Sheriff and Cherry, watch from the command center truck, parked across the street from the cousin's house. Standing by are a transport van and ambulance.

"Chief, I think the delay for the search warrant might have been a blessing. Better to do this in daylight when everybody can see everybody else. Less chance of mistakes."

"I hope you're right, Cherry. We need to close this now."

"Amen."

2 Astoria PD cars on Marine Drive are positioned on either side of the Finn's house. 2 Sheriff's vehicles are on Alameda Avenue, above the house. 4 officers have moved down the trail, waiting at the backyard fence with a metal door ram, shotguns and flash-bang stun grenades. An identical team stands ready in the front yard. Both teams will hit front and back doors simultaneously.

At 7:35am the signal is given.

"All teams go. Go! Go!"

There wasn't a need for rams, shotguns or grenades. The team at the back door saw the first body when they got on the porch. The team at the front door found it unlocked, the second body just beyond the door.

"Command, it's a nightmare in here. 2 males, both dead, each stabbed numerous times. Blood everywhere. We'll need a tech team and additional ambulance for transport to the morgue."

"What the hell?" The Chief broke radio protocol.

"I'm telling you Chief; it's a nightmare."

"Stand down and set up a perimeter. Get all uniforms out of the house. Tech team will be there ASAP."

At Command Center, not a lot said. This was not good, not good at all. The Sheriff pulled his men off the site and left. He wanted to get away, fast and far from this screw-up.

"OK Cherry, just to be clear, the only 2 suspects in the murder of that bookkeeper are now dead. Murdered while we had patrol sitting on scene."

"Yes, that appears to be true, Chief."

"Could this get any worse?"

They both knew it could, but Cherry chose not to answer the question.

"Chief, we didn't have manpower to cover front and back. We were concerned about the 2 suspects leaving, not an intruder entering."

"Well this, this . . . . " The Chief couldn't think of anything to say.

The tech team cleared the house, Cherry, Chief Jacobs and 2 officers entered the crime scene around 9:30am. There isn't much to learn. The intruder came in the back door, stabbed one cousin, then stabbed the other and left out the back door. Prints and fiber would be processed later, but it seemed the killer had come and gone without leaving much of anything except bloody footprints and a massive amount of blood.

"Start a neighborhood canvas. I want to know if anybody saw a car they hadn't seen before parked on Alameda last night."

"Will do, Detective."

The canvas took time, but it did provide a clue.

54

THE PATROL OFFICER STOOD on a porch of a tidy house on Alameda. It was a cold, blustery evening in Astoria. He hadn't been invited indoors.

> "I was walking my dog; he likes a night with no rain, not much wind. And it was that kind of night, no rain, hardly any wind. Not like the night before__"

> "Thank you, but did you see any unusual cars last night?"

"You know I did see a car. I mentioned it to the dog. I talk to the dog since Emily passed; it's a comfort, I___"

"What kind of car?"

"A Fiat. Who in the hell drives a Fiat in Astoria? Who in the hell buys a Fiat?

"What color was the Fiat?"

"Black. Where do you take a Fiat for service? Portland? Every time you need something done? Where do you get parts? Italy?"

"2 or 4 door?"

 "2 door, little tiny thing. I don't think the dog would fit in there. I know I wouldn't?"

"Did you notice the license plate?"

"Why the hell would I notice a license plate? I was walking my dog."

55

THE 3 WAREHOUSES STAND like sentinels watching
the Columbia River from shore. Each building; 300
feet long, 150 feet wide, 35 feet tall. The warehouses
had been used as a labeling and distribution plant for
canned seafood. That company moved to Seattle.

The warehouses stood empty for 3 years.

After several starts and stops, the city of Astoria, the
owner of the warehouses and a local brewery,
reached an agreement on a win-win-win deal. The
city gave up some taxes to get a big chunk of the

waterfront working again. The warehouse owner got a white elephant off his books and the brewery got ample space at a reasonable price. One warehouse will be used for brewing, one for labeling and one for distribution and a tasting room and restaurant.

Looking north across the Columbia River to Washington state, the warehouses have a million-dollar view. Not needed for brewing or distribution but ideal for a tasting room and restaurant.

A win for all involved, including the Astoria Police Department.

Little remodeling was needed at the warehouses. The former and new businesses were similar. Just different products; beer instead of fish.

2 things that did need updating were the fire control and security systems. But it turned out the security system the old company had installed still worked. Security cameras had been recording the outside of the warehouses and surrounding area for the last 3 years. The system would record for 2 weeks, erase and start over.

"It still works? Wow, that's a 10-grand savings right there. Are you sure?" The owner of the brewery is talking to the foreman of the remodel.

"Yep, we've had it running playback all morning. Not great TV, but it works."

The foreman and owner stood, watching a large monitor that showed 6 different views. 2 cameras viewed north across the trolley tracks and Riverwalk to the River.

"Not much to see, just people going by on the Riverwalk in the daytime. At night, a couple of drunks throwing up, a couple of lovers doing it on the trolley tracks."

The owner was beginning to wonder how long the foreman had been watching this.

"Doing it on the tracks seems a little uncomfortable to me. I'd__"

"Wait, what was that?"

"What? Where?"

The owner pointed at one of the views;

"Right there, on the pier, damn now it's gone. Can we rewind this?"

They could rewind, but it took a good hour to figure out how.

"OK watch closely, what are they getting out of that car?"

"Well, it's big, it could be anything, but if I had to bet, I'd say a body."

The owner, thinking the same thing.

"Look now, see it?"

They both saw it; 2 people getting a body out of the back of a small car and throwing it in the river, then 1 person pushes the other into the river.

"He gets shoved in the river."

"I think he gets knifed before he gets shoved. Rewind it, let's look again."

"You're right, stabbed, then shoved."

"Call the police."

56

CHIEF JACOBS AND CHERRY WATCHED the warehouse recording for the 5th time.

"This is the last night the dishwasher was seen alive. Right?"

"Actually, early morning of the next day Chief, according to the time stamp 3:37am."

"So, 2 people throw a body into the River, then 1 stab's the other and pitches them in?" The chief said this as a question.

"Yes sir."

"Fun bunch."

"Not really, Chief."

"So, this is a new murder, right? For a total of 5?"

"It appears so. 2 murders we're looking at here, the 2 cousins and the bookkeeper."

"Cherry, could the councilman have been the body in the car?"

"Not sure. Don't know if we'll ever find out."

"What kind of car is that?"

"A black Fiat, Chief."

"Who the hell drives a Fiat?"

"I don't know, but we'll find out."

"How in the hell do you get a dead body in a Fiat?"

"I was wondering how you get a dead body out of a Fiat."

"Can you read the license plate?"

"No, I can't, I've got the techs coming to see if they can work their magic on it."

"Thank you, Detective. Keep me posted."

"Will do, Chief."

57

THE LICENSE PLATE on the black Fiat didn't get any easier to read. Astoria PD tech team tried for a day but didn't make any headway. They did get it downloaded so it could be emailed to the State Police lab in Salem.

> "I'm not emailing anything; I'm taking the flash-drive down there myself and I'm not leaving until I get the plate number."

> "Need a driver, Chief?"

"Good idea Cherry."

The Chief and Cherry got to the Oregon State Police Lab in record time. Chief Jacobs called State Patrol to let them know there would be a high-speed Astoria PD unit heading to Salem. Lights, and when they needed it, siren. Cherry did the driving.

This is fun; she thought as they roared through the Coast Range summit on Highway 26. Big spruce trees lining the highway went by in a green blur. She was going 92 in a 55-mph zone. She liked the curvy parts of the road the best.

> "Jeesus, you must have gone to some elite driving school, Cherry."

> "Nope."

> "Where'd you learn to drive like this?"

> "Afghanistan. I can go faster if you want."

> "Good God, no, I just want you to stay on the road."

> "I can go a lot faster and stay on the blacktop; I'm holding back because I don't want you to have a heart attack. You're looking a little pale."

> "I'm fine, Cherry. I just want to get to Salem in one piece."

"Will do, Chief." She pushed the speed up to
98.

Getting the license numbers took forever. It was one
letter or numeral at a time. Each took an hour. State
Lab would have put this on the back burner if not for
the shit-storm tantrum the Astoria Police Chief threw.
Despite the histrionics of Chief Jacobs, it was Cherry
that got things moving. She didn't raise her voice or
say much; it's the vibe this attractive, uniformed cop
gave off. Confident, professional, with a hint of
violence just below the surface. It seemed she could
get physical in a second. Physical, not in a good way.

It was clear to everyone Cherry Johnson is not
someone to be messed with.

After 3 hours of waiting and watching, Cherry and the
Chief left. Lab techs had half of the plate numbers
and said they might be able to get the full license by
matching numbers they had with registered black
Fiats. They also suggested if Chief Jacobs and Cherry
left now, they would be in Astoria when the car's
owner and residence became known.

Lunch became the deciding factor; the Astorian's
were starving. Oregon State Police Lab gave them a
coupon for lunch at Ruby Tuesday's. They offered the
free lunch as an effort towards inter-agency law
enforcement support and to get them the hell out of
their hair.

After a quick, badly needed lunch, Cherry and her boss headed back to Astoria.

"No need for lights or siren, Cherry."

"How about on 217?" This is a notoriously slow, congested connecter freeway between I-5 and Highway 26.

"OK, you're right. Yes, on 217, but after that, no."

Cherry smiled to herself, *what was the point of having flashing lights, siren, if you didn't use them?*

58

10:30PM – THE NEXT DAY.

State Lab identified the owner of the black Fiat as Maylen Fisher, with an address on 5th Street between Harrison and Irving. The address was a tiny apartment down steep stairs under a small mid-century house.

Lt. Cherry Johnson had a patrol cruiser parked on 5th Street a block away from the address but with a good view. An unmarked car sat a half a block closer and an officer in plain clothes posted in the woods at the dead-end of 5th. Another officer sat in the backyard of a house directly across from the apartment.

All officers involved were on the same radio channel, radio's silenced, ear-buds in.

"All stations report."

Each officer confirmed their position to Lt. Johnson.

"Listen up. This could be a long night of waiting. The suspect car is not here, but she could be inside. Unless the suspect arrives or comes out, we stay put. For safety's sake we wait for morning to enter the apartment. At first light we will execute the warrant."

There would be no screw-ups this night.

And there were none, but they didn't get Maylen. She didn't come home. She'd had a premonition that things were closing in on her. Maylen had the same feelings in other towns.

After she left work that day, Maylen drove her Fiat the short distance to Astoria's best hotel. It sits serenely on a pier above the Columbia River; the hotel painted a regal red, stands just feet from the Columbia River shipping lanes. Ships, some over 600 feet-long, glided by the windows and rooms of the hotel. In peak tourist season, the hotel was packed.

Maylen checked into a room with a great view. This extravagance she felt she deserved. She could have left town today at the end of her shift. But wanted to pick up her paycheck tomorrow. She'd need the money; hadn't packed or taken anything from her apartment. The apartment felt unsafe now; she couldn't go back.

Maylen watched the sun drain out of the sky and fall into the Columbia, where the River reached the Pacific.

She sat in her room as the sky darkened; alone, composed and confident.

59

CHERRY TALKED TO THE OWNER of the apartment and small house above it the day before, on a phone call. She'd told the elderly lady they needed information about her tenant, Maylen Fisher, regarding a police matter.

The woman, Mrs. Hill, was forthcoming about her tenant. Yes, she had given Maylen Fisher a personal information form and lease to fill out. But she realized she must have misplaced it or not gotten it back. But not to worry, Maylen Fisher was the perfect renter. Quiet and she paid the rent on time, sometimes early.

"Such a nice young lady, never a problem. She made me the nicest cookies every week."

Now at 6am the next day, Cherry banged, hard, on the woman's door.

"Mrs. Hill, we need the key to the apartment."

"Can you come back later?" The 70-something lady clutched her dressing gown tightly.

"No ma'am. We need the key now; we don't want to break the door down."

"Break the door down, why would you do that?"

"We need the key, now."

Mrs. Hill stared past Cherry at the 3 strong men behind her, uniformed, with helmets and visors pulled down over their faces. Behind them flashing blue lights and more police cars than she could count. She had never been so frightened. She got the key.

The apartment was small, a studio with a built-in kitchenette and an unbelievably small bathroom/shower. Tastefully furnished in a very sparse, semi-Asian manner. Walls painted a pale orange; the drapes a darker rust. The bed, a futon, now folded upright to make a couch. There were no chairs in the room.

"When you have friends over, where do they sit?"

"They sit on pillows, the ones over in the corner. It's Japanese. Their interior culture is a floor culture." This came from patrolman Hal Evans.

"Hal, you have an amazing knowledge about the quirkiest things."

"I know, Cherry. My wife says it's freakish."

The search of the apartment didn't take long, not much to search. Maylen Fisher's clothes hung on a short rod on the back wall. Underneath that, 5 pairs of shoes and a small rolling suitcase. The bathroom held the usual toiletries, shampoo, toothbrush. The kitchenette was equally sparse, only mineral water in the tiny refrigerator, a box of rice crackers on the shelves above the sink.

"Man, this chick lives light."

"She sure does, but if she's on the run, she's doing it even lighter. Most of her stuff seems to be here."

And then they hit the jackpot. A small chest of drawers, maybe 3 feet tall, sat on the floor. It looked like a picture of Buddha should sit on top.

"It's a tea chest. The Japanese use it to store tea and other valuables," Hal again.

"Thank you, Hal, I'm beginning to agree with your wife."

The 6 drawers in the chest were small and square. In the first drawer, they found 3 Houston driver licenses.

"I've got a real bad feeling about this. Call the station; give them the names and addresses. Have somebody call Houston PD, find out what happened to these people."

"Will do."

The next drawer had 2 licenses, this time from Norman, Oklahoma.

The third drawer had a business card from a realtor in Tacoma, Washington, along with what appeared to be a love letter to Maylen from an Ed Davis. The postmark on the letter, from Burien, Washington.

All the names were called into the station and inquiries went out to the respective Police Departments.

The next 2 drawers held everyday things; stamps, paper clips, recipes torn out of magazines.

In the last drawer lay a figurine of a blue ox. The word 'Oregon' hand-lettered across the ox's side.

> "Wait a minute, let me look at that. I saw something like this at the murder site on Marine Drive." The senior patrolman held the ox in his gloved hand.

> "There was a Paul Bunyan salt-shaker on the mantle. It said Astoria across the bottom. I wondered where the Blue Ox was. Still can't figure out what Paul and Blue Ox have to do with Astoria."

In the same drawer, a name tag that said *Ricky Alvarez*, with the Astoria Steak Deluxe! logo below the name. Also, in the drawer was a business card from one of Astoria's City Councilmen. The Steak Deluxe! name tag for *Maylen Fisher* was in the drawer as well.

Immediately Cherry went to her radio.

> "Lights and siren to Steak Deluxe! Looking for murder suspect Maylen Fisher. Consider armed and very dangerous. All units respond."

Cherry left the apartment at a dead run. She called Steak Deluxe! from the patrol car.

60

MAYLEN LEFT HER CAR at the hotel and walked to the restaurant. At 5:30am, just beginning to get light. A nice short walk; refreshing, energizing.

At Steak Deluxe! she made herself a cup of coffee and started getting ingredients for the evening's desserts. She enjoyed this part of baking, the organization, planning, the exactness of the measurements. Baking recipes are a formula, not like cooking, where the ingredients and measures seem mere suggestions.

She was working, humming softly when Charlie came in.

"Whoa, you're here early!"

'Charlie is the only adult who uses the word whoa,' Maylen smiled to herself.

"Hi Charlie, I am here early and I need to ask 2 favors."

"Sure, what do you need?"

"May I please have my check this morning? I need to get it in the bank before the check I wrote bounces."

"Can do, you still write checks?"

"I guess I'm old fashioned that way. The other favor is more of an emergency. One of my teeth is killing me, I'm afraid it's an abscess."

"Yikes, that sounds bad."

'And he's the only adult that says yikes.'

"Thanks, the dentist said I could see him at 11:30, but I need to get the check in the bank first. I can get all of the desserts done by 10:30."

"OK, I'll get your check, you get the desserts done. It should work."

"Thanks Charlie."

While Charlie checked her timecard and wrote the paycheck, the phone rang. He let it ring; anything this early had to be a problem. He hadn't even finished his first cup of coffee.

"Here you go," Charlie said as he passed her the check. "What are the desserts tonight?"

"Tiramisu, of course. A strawberry ganache cake, and an apple, bacon, cheddar pie."

"Whoa, what's with the apple pie?"

The phone rang again.

"The test pie is in the cooler, go try it."

Charlie grabbed a dessert plate and fork, left and came back with a huge hunk of pie.

"Man-O-Man! This is good pie. Who knew a savory apple pie would be good?"

"Thanks, Charlie. I thought you would like it."

The phone rang again.

Charlie picked up the phone on the 13th ring, after he'd finished the pie.

"Hello, Steak Deluxe! . . . . . yes, yes, it is. Yes, she happens to be . . . . . what? . . . . when? . . . .

Charlie looked at Maylen, she returned his stare.

"Are you sure . . . . I can't believe . . . . I just . . . ." he hung the phone back up on the wall.

Charlie turned back to look at Maylen.

61

CHARLIE'S MIND HAD STOPPED working for a minute, then it came rushing back.

"I can't believe it."

"I know, Charlie. It will be all right". Maylen looked at Charlie directly. Her eyes didn't waiver.

"All right? All right? No, it won't be all right. You killed people."

"I know Charlie, I did," Maylen said softly. "I have 2 moods, kind and kill."

"But why . . . but wh_"

"Because I could," Maylen whispered. "Because I could."

She had moved closer to him. Charlie still had to lean in to hear her soft voice.

"Everything will be OK, Charlie."

"No, not now, that was the police. They're on their way. You're going to jail for a long time."

"I'm not so sure, Charlie. I'm not in jail yet."

Charlie didn't notice the knife until it was deep in his chest.

BORN AND RAISED IN ASTORIA, OREGON, Jim
Hallaux lives there with his wife, Robbie Mattson, and
their dog Oak.

Made in the USA
Columbia, SC
20 June 2022